SUCCULENT MEMORIES

By
Constantine Tsiftsis

Translated from Greek
By
Helen Politis

Cover: Methexis Editions
Editing: Constantine Tsiftsis

© Copyright Methexis Editions 2019
Argyroupoleos 14, 55131, Kalamaria, Greece
Tel-FAx +30 2310-278301
e-mail: info@metheksis.gr
www.metheksis.gr

Author: Constantine Tsiftsis

ISBN: 978-618-5226-89-3

To my brother Dimitri

Come on guys, let's eat, I yelled over the jazz playing on the stereo in the living room where Fanouris, Panos and Elias were sitting. Just between you and me, I called them under the pretext that the *gemista,* the stuffed tomatoes and peppers I had prepared, would get cold, which was actually true, but it just so happens, jazz really gets on my nerves, shakes up my whole bloody nervous system. I can't stand it. Whether it's *cool jazz* or *hot jazz.* It beats me how some of my friends had taken to this music and would listen to it every single chance they got, as if they had grown up with anything even resembling those sounds in their villages. I'm sure all they had ever listened to was traditional Greek country music!

Anyway, after having lowered the sounds of torture playing in the living room, they came into the kitchen with its large table for four so we could eat in peace and not gag on our food.

Sitting down at the table, I served my delicious steaming *gemista,* stuffed with rice and herbs, the Lenten version, without ground meat. That's the way I like them. I had prepared 7 stuffed tomatoes and 2 green peppers. Not too large. Not too small. That's all. I don't stuff other vegetables. To prepare the filling I scooped out the flesh of the tomatoes, careful, however, to keep the outer layer and the skin intact. Then I finely chopped some parsley, a bit of fresh dill and mint for flavor, also adding some currents and pine nuts we had from back home. For an even greater flavor boost, I threw in plenty of finely diced spring onions and a couple of cloves of crushed garlic. Then I added fluffy long grain rice along with the pith and seeds from the peppers, as well as a generous amount of ketchup instead of the traditional sugar I had seen my grandmother use. Finally, I pierced the peppers in a few places with a fork, while my secret for success was to add, as a final touch to the filling, some grated sharp, salty yellow cheese and a generous amount of olive oil. I remember my grandmother always muttering when she used to pour olive oil by the bottleful over her *gemista:* 'Stewed vegetables need their olive oil,' she would say. The rest was a pinch of salt, freshly ground black pepper, and a bit of ginger along with another secret ingredient of mine, some very spicy Mexican hot sauce, just 'the tip of a spoon's worth.' Without exaggeration, the result was a scrumptious feast! At the table, we also had fresh bread and feta cheese, even though the feta wasn't the real thing.

Fanouris, a dark-haired, tall and handsome young man, around 6'3", with brown eyes and a piercing gaze, a wonderful smile, straight teeth, full lips, was from a village outside Kozani, a town in northern Greece. He was the son of an Orthodox priest and was studying what he had always wanted to - electronic engineering. He had not bothered to take the university entrance exams in Greece, opting instead to study abroad, as electronics was an unknown field in Greece at the time. Fanouris only ate stuffed tomatoes.

Then there was Elias, from Kavalla, another town in northern Greece - average height, a swarthy complexion, stocky, with eyes black as tar and black hair straight as an arrow - who was awesome at the gift of the gab, wearing you down until you finally surrendered and agreed with him. He was studying business management. Finally, last but not least, there was Panos, from Thebes, a town near Athens, also of average height, blue-eyed, with brownish blond hair, soft-spoken, slightly overweight, who wore wire-rimmed prescription glasses that really suited him. He was a Ph.D. student in chemistry.

Unlike Fanouris, Elias and Panos had no prejudices; they ate everything.

I don't suppose I've mentioned I also know how to cook, did I? I can't imagine how that slipped my mind! Sorry about that.

Well, then, listen to this. As a kid, and when I say kid, I mean the first grades of grammar school, I usually did my homework at the kitchen table, because the kitchen was the warmest room in the whole house. While I studied, my mother and my grandmother cooked, when they didn't have ironing to do or some other household task that could be carried out elsewhere in the house. The range of their culinary repertoire was not, let us say, huge. The menu was a bit - or rather, very predictable... Twice a week stews - ah that wonderful olive oil! - usually on Wednesdays and Fridays. One day it would be beans, one day fish, if available, and twice a week meat. Once a week, usually every Thursday, the fridge would be cleared out and it would be leftovers, or something quick and easy to prepare like potatoes with eggs, or tomatoes with eggs, or even eggs on their own, and if we were really lucky, one of those amazing, mouth-watering homemade pies that I still dream about today, with layer upon layer of hand-rolled phyllo pastry, crisp and crunchy with every bite, baked to perfection in our wood-fired oven back home. The days we had meat were always Tuesdays and Sundays. Tuesday was usually a dish with chicken and either rice or fried potatoes, and other times something with ground meat, like spaghetti with meat sauce or meatballs, or even *dolmadakia* - stuffed cabbage rolls with ground meat and rice, or *youvarlakia* - meatballs in a lemon-egg cream sauce. In the summertime we'd have *moussaka,* and on holidays and anniversaries, *pastitsio.* On Sundays, *youvetsi* - meat with orzo and tomato. Beans and pulses were always available. One of my favorites was *fava* - yellow split peas which were boiled and mashed, almost into a paste, drizzled with olive oil, which, I remember, was always served with a bowl of finely diced onions, freshly squeezed lemon juice, and olives. I also loved *fakes* - lentil soup, and various other beans. But I never liked *revithia* – chickpeas - never liked the way they were prepared. Now, after Sifnos, Paros, and Iphigenia (not necessarily in that order), I grew to like them. By the way, for those not in the know, Iphigenia is my lovely wife and a terrific cook, better than my mother, even rivalling my grandmother.

So while I sat studying at the kitchen table, I was exposed to all the goings-on as the meals were being prepared, without realizing that I was actually recording these procedures and recipes. Absorbing them subconsciously, in such a way that I was able to reproduce them perfectly! Of course, I didn't discover this until I was a graduate student studying abroad and was on the verge of dying of starvation. That's when I realized that I was capable of staying both alive and well-fed. Well-fed without spending much, while at the same time, assuming the role of guardian angel for a few stupid guys like myself in the beginning, who thought that food away from home was only available either in diners or as part of the occasional care packages in brightly-colored Tupperware that would arrive from that magical faraway place called the 'homeland', inhabited by those mythical creatures called 'mothers'.

Truth be told, those first two to three weeks of practicing my culinary skills were more like a period of transition between total starvation and survival. Taste and quality of food in the dishes I cooked played a secondary role. The objective was survival. Over time, however, my 'house' became synonymous with 'good food'. There was always someone or other who would drop by unexpectedly, claiming they just happened to be in the neighborhood. And inevitably, they were always hungry. Normally, at our place there were about six people who ate there regularly. Three Greeks, one Greek Cypriot and two foreigners. Sometimes there were other hangers-on. Later, we established a system of BYOF. Whoever ate had to bring something from the supermarket that we had asked for, or he didn't come back. We had no use for freeloaders, and he would be blacklisted. And as for my cooking, I was even almost mentioned in the local press. A cousin of my Turkish friend Murat-Erke who also happened to be a frequent guest at my table, as well as a journalist at a local newspaper, ate a *tas kebab* I had prepared with a fluffy rice pilaf that blew his mind! Then there was another friend, a fellow graduate student, a mathematician like me, who hailed from Mexico City, Jesus by name, who resembled a flamenco dancer in the way he moved - tall, thin, and handsome, dark, with long sideburns and hair, with a perpetual fire in his eyes. One day, while we were studying together, I served up a dish I had prepared. A freshly baked, steaming *pastitsio*, a casserole with macaroni and ground beef cooked with a special twist, with cinnamon and allspice, topped with a luscious layer of creamy béchamel to die for. It knocked his socks off! I couldn't get rid of him that night. He just wouldn't leave. He only complied when I handed him a doggie bag containing three sizeable servings of my *pastitsio*. Needless to say, he came by the house one day with his sister Amalia in tow. She had come to visit him and he had brought her over so we could cook a *pastitsio* together. He had given her orders to write down the recipe in every minute detail. By the way, *kanella*, the Greek word for cinnamon, happens to be the same in Spanish. Did you know that? Do you see how many new things you can learn by reading me?

Then there was my Cypriot friend, Philippos Philippou, an only child from Limassol, a Ph.D. student in biology, who always brought us *haloumi,* a well-known Cypriot cheese, whenever he came by. He was a tall guy, quiet and soft spoken, with curly brown hair, black almond shaped eyes, a perfect set of teeth and handsome features. His English was excellent. He was shy, but good company. He wore glasses with tortoise shell frames that gave him a somewhat aristocratic air. His father was a judge and his mother a lawyer with the Ministry of Justice in Cyprus. We used to kid him quite a bit because of his double name.

Even though he had a driver's license, and an international one at that, Philippos never drove. Eventually, I got him to tell me why. He had learned to drive on the left side of the road, as they do in Cyprus and the UK, and was afraid to drive on the right, afraid he might have an accident. I mentioned this to Fanouris and we joked around about it. One day, as we chatted over dinner with Philippos, Panos and Elias, Elias asked Philippos why he didn't drive. Fanouris promptly butted in, telling them that Philippos couldn't drive a car with the steering wheel on the left. When Elias asked why, Fanouris said *Because every time he goes to change gears, he accidentally opens the car door instead, and it scares him shitless!* I remember how we all cracked up!

I received my master's in philosophy- with honors - in just fifteen months. I kid you not – I really did! At which point, all my 'clients' and 'messmates' fell all over me, each one of them with a litany of sound arguments, to try and convince me to stay on for a PhD. They all wanted me to stick around in that godforsaken place for at least two more years so they wouldn't starve to death! I dumped the lot of them and left anyway.

I never found out until recently, some 35 years later, when I ran into Fanouris, what had become of all those guys I used to feed and had left behind. Over the years, most of us had lost touch. Actually, there hadn't been too many of us. All had managed to survive without me, one way or another. At that time, money had been tight and it wasn't possible to make ends meet if one ate out. I had discovered that very early on. In any case, you didn't have to be the brightest bulb in the room to get it. Your stomach was a constant reminder.

Those boys, in true Greek fashion, had been raised by their mamas to have everything handed to them, as if they were incapable of thinking or doing anything for themselves. Typical endearments would be along the lines of *Don't tire yourself, my little satrap, you're a man! Mama's here to make you whatever your little heart desires,* or words to that effect, turning them all into fucking useless lumps. They were no good with their hands, couldn't do even the simplest task without making a mess of it. Like boiling water! Sometimes, I think that the women they eventually married must have cursed their mothers-in-law many a time. You see, Greek mothers who raise boys, do so in such a way that not even they themselves would ever consider marrying them! Another important point is that they don't bring them up to have any goals in life. Maybe they should start with the simplest one - toilet training!

Moreover, some of the guys, fortunately only a handful, played it very macho, and didn't look kindly on my preoccupation with cooking and household chores in general. But, naturally, I had no intention of living in a pigsty. Anyway, I didn't give a damn about what every idiot thought or said, as long as my stomach was full and my personal space clean and neat. Because I wasn't afraid of making fun of myself, I'd hang around the student union at the university with my friends, describing loudly and in great detail all the chores I had done that morning around the house. I'd tell them how I had done my own laundry, ironed my clothes, sewed on buttons that were missing, and spent plenty of time in the kitchen, cooking. Then I had swept the house, mopped and dusted. All this time, two guys who were from Crete - and it was always the same two guys - would stare at me aghast as if I were some strange being from outer space.

In the silence that would inevitably ensue, I'd crack a smile and say:

Then I stopped, because I was expecting my period and had bad cramp!

This was met with roars of laughter from my friends, while the two Cretans weren't sure how to react, and just sat there awkwardly, unsure whether to laugh or not.

Sometime later, they both dropped by for a visit one afternoon with my good friend Panos who was doing a graduate degree in chemistry. To make a long story short, we all sat down to enjoy my special *gigantes* bean casserole that I had prepared with bacon and an extra dose of garlic. I had sautéed onions together with the garlic in Greek virgin olive oil from far-off Sparta, that miraculously, I had found at our local supermarket, and had grated three ripe tomatoes which I added to the beans along with some fresh dill for flavor, and a generous dose of freshly-ground black pepper. The dish was accompanied by warm freshly-baked bread from the corner bakery, olives from Kalamata, sent to Fanouris by his father in Greece - will talk further on that subject a bit later - and imitation feta from the grocery store run by Luigi, a roly-poly third generation Italian-American whose family was originally from Modena. To drink, we had some of those icy-cold bland American beers, brought by our visitors, and we just chilled. From then on, they never again made any derogatory comments. On the contrary, Manousos, a chubby guy of average height, blue-eyed with a thick mane of reddish-blond hair, one of the two Cretans graduating from med school, asked me confidentially one day if I would give him some basic pointers on how he could beat his hunger! I gladly showed him some very basic cooking skills that would help keep him alive. I remember at some point asking him if he wanted me to show him how to make a spaghetti with meat sauce. He told me he never ate that stuff. I couldn't believe it and I lost it!

Hey, man! Why didn't you just spit it out from the start that you're nuts?! I said.

He simply stared back at me blankly, bewildered.

What is it you don't get? I asked.

He had nothing to say.

Many years later, purely by chance, we ran into each other at the Evangelismos Hospital in central Athens where Manousos was a resident ORL. He confessed that, at home, he was the one who did the cooking, because his wife who was also a doctor, a pediatrician at the Agia Sofia children's hospital, was clueless in the kitchen. He also confided that never had he ever had such tasty *gigantes* as the ones he had eaten at my house all those years ago. I told him they really hadn't been particularly special, that most likely it was hunger that had made him gobble them down with such an appetite and that's why to him they remained unforgettable. I told him the Germans had a saying, *Hunger ist die beste Köchin;* in other words, hunger is the best cook. He agreed wholeheartedly.

Beyond the matter of hunger however, there was another unresolved problem which harassed all of us students in those days. Sex. And when we say unresolved, boy, do we mean it! More so in Greece and a little less abroad. No joke. In Greece, as students, to get to score a girl you had to do cartwheels, and even then, it was no easy feat. Elsewhere, also tough. In fact, those of us who made the mistake of going to Italy for postgraduate studies, especially in the smaller towns outside the big cities - Rome, Bologna, Naples or Milan - they really got screwed - or rather, didn't! The situation was pretty much the same as in Greece. Those students who returned home either came back sex-starved or married! Though some did remain abroad. Those who went further north, beyond the 50th parallel, fared better, at least in that respect. For us, on the other hand, the ones who switched continents, the situation was even crazier. It couldn't have been worse. You see, I went to a shithole of a town in one of the south-central states, where in addition to religious fanaticism and ignorance, one had to deal with narrow-minded conservative attitudes. However, in our specific fields, it was a top university. All told, we were a group of only 8 or 10 Greeks, and another 4 or 5 Greek-Cypriots, at a humongous university in a one-horse town. A few of the guys used to gather for meals at my house. To meet girls - a rare commodity in our particular disciplines at the university, and the few attending might as well not have existed - some of us signed up for Sunday School at the Greek church, spurred on by Fanouris. That's a fact. Fanouris, as the son of a priest, knew all the ins and outs and after a bit of research had found out that there actually was a Greek Orthodox church in town, Saint George, that offered catechism classes every Wednesday and Sunday afternoons, and that they were very popular among the young women of the Greek-speaking community. It took Fanouris about a week to pass on this information to us, as every time he tried to mention catechism or Sunday School, he'd get ragged half to death!

We finally decided to go ahead and give it a try, to see what was in play. The classes were divided into two groups. The first was for the very young set, kiddies up to 16, maybe stretching it to 17 max. The other, supposedly the advanced class from ages 16 on up, until around 20. So the guys decided to join the second group, thinking that as the girls were 'advanced', surely, they must have heard something about 'original sin'. Also, they would not be at risk from the cops, in case something was to go wrong. Personally, as a graduate student myself, at the ripe old age of 24, I was considered 'over the hill' for this age group. I was more suited to chasing after Asimina, the hot cleaning lady of the church who was also in charge of lighting the candles and who had a roving eye. Whatever. More on that later. So, finally three of the guys signed up. Fanouris, Petros and Elias. To make a long story short, two of them really fucked up. Petros, a blond, good-looking young guy from Karditsa, a town in central Greece - tall, with large green eyes, who played the guitar and sang beautifully, married before finishing his degree because he knocked up his girlfriend. This put an abrupt end to his studies in pharmacology. He moved in with his in-laws and began work at his father-in-law's diner. Elias, on the other hand, left in the dead of night, moving to another state. Fanouris was the only one to remain unscathed. At the very last minute, he didn't marry the beautiful Lillian, because someone else beat him to it: an American, her old boyfriend from high school. As for myself, the closest I got to having sex at the time was jumping from one subject to another.

Those years were tough. Just to give you an idea, the greatest technological innovations at the time were the bicycle and the transistor radio.

Naturally, getting a car was out of the question! Even though it was one of those absolute necessities. Something you couldn't do without. If you didn't have a car, you were really done for. Distances were huge. Everything was miles away from wherever you happened to be. (Not only everything, but every living being, too). Without your own car, you'd waste at least two hours a day in travel time and delays, come rain or shine, depending naturally on where you were going. Without a car, you felt like an outcast. Always at the mercy of one person or another who had a car, begging for a ride, if there happened to be room in the car for an extra person and, of course, whether or not they liked you. Girlfriends, dating? Out of the question. Without a car, you were akin to a leper. As soon as they found out you didn't have a car, no one came near you. For instance, if you hit on a girl you took a shine to, and she happened to like you too, she'd ask you to 'come by my house to pick me up' - even if she lived 35 miles away on the other side of town! And most probably, she'd even have a car of her own. But the conservative attitudes, the provinciality of the 'heartland', would not allow her to come pick *you* up. It was unbelievable. That was the man's role. So you had to go pick her up, take her out on the date, then take her back home, before heading back to your own place, hopefully without getting lost. Fuck it. Cars, especially all types of used cars, depending on their condition, ranged in price from very cheap to very expensive. You could find whatever you wanted. And the saying 'what you pay for is what you get' certainly applied in this case. As far as I was concerned, after the first month, I realized that without a car I'd be lost. I couldn't have any kind of a social life. Or anything else. My choices were either to live in the center of town, where rents were sky high, or live in the student dorms on the college campus, cut off from everything, forced to hang out with all the assholes living there. Which is finally what I did. At that time, there were no mixed dorms, as there are today. Then it was either men or women. Or fraternities or sororities. That was it. In the beginning, I was accepted into the IΦΘ fraternity. It was great, but just for a short while. To start with, everyone there, about 24 guys, were absolute psychos, obsessed with American football. I, on the other hand, who was into basketball and soccer – real football - was considered a pariah or just plain weird. Most of the guys there were undergraduates in various fields of engineering. However, they were all pretty useless at math. That's where I got even. Took my revenge. Eventually, one by one, or in groups, they came to me to solve their various math problems, be it calculus or differential equations or complex functions of probabilities. Depending on the year they were in. At first, I was glad to help. Later on, with my rapid increase in clientele, this began to be a bit of a strain, affecting my own work. So I told them the tutoring would no longer be free, it would cost them $6.00 an hour. Very cheap, if you consider a beer at the bar cost about $1.35 a bottle. Immediately, business dropped off. A few did remain and I managed to make some decent pocket money. Most of the time, I hung out with Fanouris, who lived next door at the ΣAE house, about 150 feet away. He was younger, just turned 19, but was a blast to be with. Being a blast is great, as long as it's not thermonuclear.

Fanouris had two older sisters, both happily married. His mother, of Egyptian origin, was a graduate in English literature and an English teacher with a preparatory school of her own in his hometown of Kozani. According to what Fanouris had implied, she was very well off financially, even though she gave the poor bastard a bad time, claiming he spent money thoughtlessly, and needed to learn to live with less and to budget more carefully. Bullshit, if you want my opinion. This is something you teach your child when you have him close to you, still under your wing. *Not* when you send him off to the ends of the earth. You've got to think of what would happen to your child if something went wrong. He should always have a safety net to fall back on.

Fanouris was in the process of negotiating the purchase of a secondhand Audi 100. Once, he told me, when I had asked, that he wanted 'a small car'. I remember telling him to only buy a car he could push. I never quite understood how a car with a 2000cc engine could be classified as 'small'. America, you see, is a country where a sense of measure is nonexistent. There, you can see the tallest people you've ever seen in your life, and the shortest. The fattest and the thinnest. The tallest buildings in the world and the largest cars. The most beautiful designer clothes and shoes, as well as the most god-awful ones, reflecting the worst possible taste, pure kitsch. The richest people in the world as well as the poorest, the penniless. Everyone coexists without any sense of measure. Accordingly, when someone tells you he has a small car, it could very well be 3,500 cc's since their 'large' cars could be 15,000 cc's or more. You see, there, they measure engine size in cubic inches. So when you hear of a car with an 800 engine, quoted in inches, that's equivalent to 12,000 cubic centimeters. No one really cares since the cost of gas there is practically nothing. What one liter of gas costs in Greece, is equivalent to the cost of one gallon in the US - which is four liters, more or less.

Finally, Fanouris bought the car, and if I remember correctly, for $350. It had clocked 60,000 miles. It looked good, bright red with a black stripe on the side, beige leather interior and brand new tires. Awesome. We took photos to send back home to the 'village' and went into town to drink a beer for good luck. The car was not an automatic and had a short gear shift with five gears. I noticed that at traffic lights, Fanouris was stepping down on both the brake and clutch at the same time, which in the long run would wear out the disc. I said to him:

Put it in neutral.

What do you mean, neutral? he asked. I stared at him to see if he was kidding.

Neutral territory - no man's land, you idiot.

Because he continued to stare at me with the clever look of a cow when it sees a train speeding by, I explained what I meant. Then he got it.

We finally made it to the bar. A very hip, large venue with cool vibes and atmosphere, and a sharp barman - Mike, a tall, lanky, exuberant Irishman with long, dark, wavy hair parted in the middle, intelligent brown eyes constantly in motion, a large nose and fast-moving long arms, who happened to be a really funky DJ as well, very much into his music and kind of weird, who every night, whipped the crowd up into a frenzy.

Fanouris parked the car right in front of the bar. A sign caught my eye indicating that parking there was prohibited between the hours of 7am and 7pm.

I said to him, *Don't park here, you'll get a ticket.*

What ticket? he asked.

A ticket to the Super Bowl, you moron!

He looked at me with a dumb expression. It dawned on him when I pointed out the no parking sign, and he moved the car. Fortunately for him, because right after that, the cops did show up.

See, you idiot? You just made it. By a split second. This isn't Kozani, where you can park wherever you bloody well please, or, if they write you up, the village priest gets you off the hook, I said. Over here the cops are cops, they don't cruise around for chicks or stop for a gyro souvlaki.

While drinking our beers at the bar with Mike, a thought came to me in a flash.

Hey man, you got a license? I asked Fanouris.

What license? he asked back.

License to kill, you loser. A driver's license, man. D'you have one?

Sure, he says, showing me his Greek license. I couldn't believe it!

Damn, how dense can you be? I said. *You country bumpkin, don't you have an international driver's license?*

He had no idea what that was. I showed him mine and explained what it was. To make a long story short, both Mike and I told him that if he were stopped by the cops, he would no longer have a car, because they'd impound it - nor any money, as the fine he'd have to pay was three times more than the price of the car, let alone possible jail time. What he needed to do at once was apply for a state license and take the required driving test. In the meantime, until he got his local license, I would drive his car. That's what we agreed to. And so I suddenly found myself driving a bright red Audi 100 with a black stripe on the side, beige leather seats and brand new tires, as if I were the local drug dealer.

Since I now *had* a car, so to speak, I convinced Fanouris we should rent an apartment off-campus as far from the city center as possible, in a pleasant newly-developing suburb, where the rents were still comparatively dirt cheap. After a lot of searching, we found a beautiful furnished apartment, relatively new, very bright, with a living room, kitchen-dining room, two bedrooms and two baths on the second floor of a three-story building without an elevator. It was $210 a month. Don't laugh. At the time, that was quite a sum. Just to give you an idea, I was getting $370 a month from my scholarship fund, and Fanouris was receiving $330 a month from Greece, from his father the priest. But we finally had our own place, could do as we pleased, see whoever we wanted, no longer having to put up with any annoying assholes. That was a great thing. That was definitely a plus. The minus was the $105 each of us had to hand over every month for the rent, and an additional $20 or so each for utilities - phone, water, and electricity. In the dorms, we had been paying $95 a piece to the university every month, which included everything. Now, for only $60 a month more for the two of us, we were buying our peace of mind. It was well worth it.

As a flat mate, Fanouris was very easygoing and we hit it off right away. For starters, he was very clean. Both on his person as well as around the house. A big plus. And he was very tidy. Almost as tidy as I was. I never left things lying around. We had a place for everything and always put things away. He was also quiet and studious, respecting the other person's boundaries - especially my need for peace and quiet while I worked. Most of all, he loved to iron. I don't know the how and why, but he sure knew how to iron. Very professional. When I saw this for the first time, I was amazed. Kudos to him! I also ironed, but considered it a chore, and could never do it as well as he did. That's when I nicknamed him *Iron Man,* after the American comic book hero.

We got along very well. Though a few of his habits did get on my nerves. He didn't shine his shoes often enough, often forgot to turn off the coffee maker, only listened to jazz, didn't change his socks every day, was a fanatic AEK soccer fan, and farted constantly around the house.

I imagine certain idiosyncrasies of mine ticked him off too, but generally speaking, the two of us had found quite a successful *modus vivendi.*

After a couple of weeks, we thought it best to try to economize, to cut down on our expenses. We were already doing our own housework and we now decided to do our own cooking and eat in. And so began this whole story with cooking, as I mentioned earlier. Soon I was the only one doing the cooking, first of all, because I enjoyed it, and second, whenever Fanouris cooked we ended up throwing the food away. Therefore zero savings! To earn a bit of additional change, I did some private math tutoring whenever I had the chance, and Fanouris found a part-time job in the evenings at a huge supermarket nearby, that was open from 7 in the morning to midnight. He worked the 8pm to midnight shift six days a week. At midnight, I'd go pick him up in his car, and if he wasn't dead tired, we'd go get a beer at a nice bar in the area, or drop by Mike's where the cool crowd gathered. Once in a while we'd even shoot a game of pool. The good thing with the supermarket was that in addition to the not-so-generous $1.93 an hour he earned - as he didn't have a green card - they'd give him certain food items with 'almost expired' due dates, free of charge. So we ate for practically nothing. To make a long story short, after the first couple of months, we were getting by beautifully. Masters of the universe. We had money, a nice house, classy car, super-duper stereo, a phone and a color TV. All that.

Except for chicks. But we still kept looking. We were not about to give up.

After that, came the phase with the Sunday School classes I was talking about. Fanouris got involved with Lillian, a young Greek-American girl. Her father was a second generation American of Greek descent, with roots in Kalamata, who owned a large, centrally-located dry-cleaning business downtown, and her mother was American, a teacher from Denver, Colorado. Lillian was beautiful. And when we say beautiful, we mean that if you saw her in the street, you'd do a double-take. A true goddess. You couldn't help but notice her. Tall, about 5 foot 9, with long, wavy blond hair, enormous blue eyes which took your breath away when she looked at you, and amazing breasts. As we learned later, she had even won first prize at a local beauty pageant the year before. She had just finished high school and planned to attend college the following year to study art history and anthropology. She had two younger siblings. A sister, two years younger, also gorgeous, but a brunette, and a brother who was four years younger. Fanouris, when he first saw her, was blown away. Understandably so. From that day on, he drove me crazy. He'd come home after catechism classes and couldn't stop talking about her.

I try to get her talking but she just ignores me, was the sort of thing he kept saying.

I think that's the only thing you'll ever get her to do, I'd answer, thinking of the righteous conservatism of the region, bursting his bubble, trying to talk some sense into him.

But I really like her a lot, she's so beautiful, he'd respond, going on and on about her.

I tried explaining that beauty, when not accompanied by other basic human characteristics, was great only for marble statues, but he wouldn't listen to me.

Until he managed to finally get her to say 'yes' he was hell to be around. He never allowed me a moment's peace. He talked about her incessantly. Let alone the endless phone conversations he had with her. He was obsessed. Almost nothing else mattered to him anymore.

At some point, after about three weeks, he finally managed to kiss her. That did the trick. They decided to go out on a date. They arranged for Fanouris to pick her up from her house so he could meet her parents. That's how things were done there. He rushed home to tell me, overcome with excitement.,

What the blazes, you fool, I said. *How are you going to drive without a license? In two days, you're going to take the test. If the cops catch you now, what'll you do? It'll ruin everything. Did you think about that? Why don't you pick her up in a taxi instead?*

It was a waste of breath. He wouldn't listen. It was like talking to a brick wall. I backed down.

Do whatever you please, I said. *But don't blame me if things go sour.*

On Sunday, he dressed to kill. He took the car and left to go pick up Lillian. They'd first go to Sunday School class at the church and then later, to the movies. Crossing myself, I prayed he would refrain from doing something stupid behind the wheel. Because if he did, and was stopped by a traffic cop, he'd be in deep shit. Up until his return that night at 11, I must admit I was very worried. I had been waiting for the phone to ring, and a call from the police station, but fortunately nothing happened. After he came in, we poured a couple of beers and he sat down to give me the complete lowdown. God help me! Until quarter to three in the morning he talked nonstop. I was so tired I was ready to drop. I needed matchsticks to keep my eyes open! Finally I insisted it was time to turn in and that we could continue the next day.

And tomorrow's another day. We can chat again. And it's Monday to boot. A working day for both of us.

But nothing seemed to sink in. He followed me to my room and kept on talking. First about her, then about her parents, then her home, then the movie they had seen that had made such an impression on them. It was that Brando film, *The Last Tango in Paris.*

At some point, he finally left and went to his room. I conked out.

Our life changed after Lillian. Fanouris got his driver's license and turned into *Ferry*. That's what we called him from that day on, because that's what she called him. He began to neglect his studies, and his grades started to drop. Soon, he was cutting classes. One day, I remember asking him why he didn't have any classes that day. His answer was:

I did have a class today, but Lillian called me in the morning and said, 'Let's go for a coffee!' Since I went out for coffee, how could I go to class, too?

I freaked out. My god, I couldn't believe my ears! He'd completely flipped. What bullshit! Truly a lost cause. In any case, now I was forced to buy a car of my own to travel back and forth to the university. I bought a blue second-hand Buick Caravan, with automatic transmission, and 45,000 miles on it. A good deal at $400. Then, I also found a job. I started teaching math as a substitute teacher at an exclusive private school nearby. It was an instance of being in the right place at the right time. Their regular teacher had died suddenly of a heart attack at the beginning of the year and they had to fill the position immediately. I was to teach grades 8 and 9. The principal at the school had reached out to the university for help, and the professor I was working with recommended me along with two others. They ended up hiring the lot of us. The principal was a good sort, a simple soul, who informed me that he had registered me at the local branch of the Department of Health, Education and Welfare and had also filled in an application for me to receive a Social Security card. That made my head spin. Needless to say, I figured all of this was completely illegal, since as a foreigner, even though a grad student, I had absolutely no legal right to work. Therefore, I felt it was only a matter of time before the guys in trench-coats and dark glasses would show up to put me in handcuffs! The money, however, was good. It was more than $7 an hour for 8 hours per week. Curiously, those guys in trench coats I was expecting, never showed. Much later, I found out why. The principal's secretary, Mrs. Lee, a charming, redheaded Irishwoman, smart as a whip, tall, around forty-five, had a son who was a student of mine. And because she was on the ball and knew what was what, she had never officially submitted the applications to the DHEW and Social Security for me. That was how, up until June when school was out, I had managed to secure 8 months on the job with very good results; 100% of my students had done much better on their exams compared to all previous years, while around 60% had received the best grades statewide. So it seemed, after all, that I was, in fact, a very good teacher.

Meanwhile, in the two months that followed, Lillian had begun coming and going as she pleased, like the lady of the house, either alone or together with Ferry, who had given her a set of keys of her own. I got hold of Fanouris one day, sat him down, and tried to drum some sense into his head. I didn't mince words. I threatened to move out. I also told him I was determined to write to his father. This really shook him up. He promised to turn over a new leaf. Honestly, he tried really hard to do so, but the poor sod was head over heels in love, and the devil with everything else. You see, the good thing about having a chick is the sex. The bad thing - is still the sex. Fortunately, Lillian was no virgin. Her high school boyfriend had nailed her on prom night. That was how Fanouris found the road ahead open, the light green and simply went wild. I, on the other hand, had to wait for some apple to ripen and fall into my lap. I thought it was high time I took drastic action and did something about my sex life. Maybe I needed to start praying to the gods or sacrifice a lamb.

I finally made a decision, and one Sunday morning went to church. I got there around 10. It was a full house. I never expected to see so many Greeks gathered in one place in that town. In about a half hour, the service was over. Father Charalambis, sweet as could be, blond, blue-eyed, slim, was a young priest of about thirty-five or forty, with a ten-day beard, dressed in a black habit similar to that of his Catholic counterparts. He stood at the door greeting his parishioners one by one with a smile and a kind word. Then came my turn. He greeted me by name and told me how happy he was to see me there. I was blown away. Never expected that. People had now gathered outside in the churchyard, in small groups, talking. I didn't know anyone there except for Lillian who was there with her parents. She pretended not to know me. I was about to leave when Father Charalambis stopped me to chat. He knew everything about me. When I say everything, I mean everything about my studies. He took me by the arm and started introducing me left and right. He also introduced me to Lillian's parents. Everyone greeted me with a smile, and after asking me what part of Greece I was from, they all had something nice to say. Some of them were even aware that I taught at the private prep school. Some of their children attended that school. What made a special impression on me was that when I had glanced through the list of my school's students, I hadn't noticed any Greek surnames. Later, I learned that they had anglicized their names, since most were third generation Americans, or even fourth. However, everyone spoke Greek. Even if just a broken version, executed with some effort. The same applied to their children. I found that awesome. I was very proud of these people. I thought of how all of them, despite being loyal Americans to the core, still managed to retain a certain flame, a spark of the old country, the *patrida,* which was very moving. By comparison, as far as I was concerned, they were more Philhellenes than any native-born Greek. Within them truly burned the torch of Hellenism. Many of them invited me to their homes for a barbecue. Everyone wanted to make sure I didn't feel alone and miserable. I was touched. I thanked them all. They made me feel very welcome. I decided to attend church every Sunday to be together with these wonderful people.

I asked where I could get a glass of water. Father Charalambis told me to go into the church and ask Semy for one. I went back in and then realized he was referring to Asimina. She brought me a glass of water right away, then stood in front of me, staring at me intently as I was drinking. I almost choked. And then it happened. We clicked. That was it.

Semy was from Igoumenitsa, a coastal town opposite the island of Corfu northwestern of Greece, and she happened to be a real knockout. She had come to the US with her parents in '58, at the invitation of her mother's sister who had married an American in '52. Her father worked in his brother-in-law's dealership, selling car tires. Asimina, who later became Semy, at the age of nineteen married a swindler, a third generation Greek-American, with roots in Pyrgos, in the Peloponnesus. The marriage lasted about two years. When he was sentenced to 15 years in jail for forgery, she filed for divorce. Fortunately. they had no children. After her father's death, she was left all alone in the world, having already lost her mother earlier. Her aunt took her under her wing, finding a job for her at the church so she could have an income of her own, social security, and one day, a pension.

Anyway, we got to talking.

How old are you? I asked. Indiscreet on my part, but it just slipped out.

Approaching twenty-five, she replied.

From what direction? I asked, but luckily, she didn't get the humor.

She told me where she was staying. She was living with her aunt near the church. We arranged to go out on a date. I was to pick her up from her house in the afternoon, go for a drive so we could continue where we left off. Arriving on time, she suggested we visit the huge, brand new mall which had just recently opened for business. She was well-dressed for the occasion, and perfectly made up. She was a very beautiful woman. Not very tall, around 5'6", she had skin like white alabaster, thick, wavy black hair and large expressive green eyes. Beautiful pearly teeth and full, luscious lips. Neither heavy nor skinny. Just right, with curves in the right places. In any event, the mall we went to had lovely shops, bustling with people, mainly upscale clientele. I remember we sat at a coffee shop. We talked a lot. I don't remember everything we said. She told me she was from Igoumenitsa and asked me if I had ever been there. I said that I had been once on a school trip. She asked me what I had liked best about the place.

The only thing I liked about Igoumenitsa, I replied, *Was that Corfu lay directly opposite!*

She didn't seem to quite appreciate this. But because I was chuckling as I said it, she gave my arm a nudge and said:

You're kidding, aren't you?

What could I do? Naturally, I said, *Of course.*

Then she told me her mother's name was Anatoli, (Greek for 'east'). I asked if her mother had a particular liking for spices, but once again, she didn't get it. We got past that, too. We were having a good time. I suggested we go over to my place. She asked why and I said I wanted to show her my collection of little flying elephants. She laughed, and off we went.

Fanouris was out. Semy liked the apartment. I had her sit down in the living room, dimmed the lights and put on some music. A Frank Sinatra record. She was thrilled. I went into the kitchen to throw together a quick snack. Fried chicken nuggets to which I added a mustard sauce with grated anise and a bit of lime juice, together with cubed sweet potatoes with ginger. I also opened a bottle of Californian red merlot. I placed everything on a trolley, together with two long-stemmed wine glasses we had inherited from the previous tenants, paper napkins and two forks, and wheeled it into the living room. She was bowled over, the surprise on her face evident. She looked at me as if I were the Wizard of Oz. We snacked and drank the whole bottle of wine while we chatted casually, comfortably. She told me it was the first time in her life a man had ever cooked for her. She was visibly moved. A good sign. You know what they say, a glass of wine is good for the health. By extension, its only logical to assume a whole bottle of wine should work wonders. And so it did. After we had finished, I took her gently in my arms and kissed her. She was expecting it, and reciprocated without pulling away. Things just got better and better. She asked where the bathroom was. The temperature was rising dangerously, or was that simply my imagination at work? When she returned, I led her to my bedroom, and that's where we stayed.

I can't even remember the number of times we made love.

You've heard how lots of people tend to light up a cigarette after sex? Well, I lit a huge torch to the Virgin Mary the very next day!

While we lay in bed in each other's arms, recuperating during much-needed timeouts, we talked about so many things. We jumped from one subject to the other. Randomly. You know what I'm referring to, what we call small talk after sex. I imagine somehow this was how philosophy was born, as the ancient Greeks had no cigarettes to smoke after sex. She asked me about mathematics. Why I did what I did at the university. I answered that I loved the subject, and that my particular field was applied mathematics in engineering. I explained that mathematics is the science that studies subjects that deal with quantity (in other words, numbers), structures (in other words, form), space, change, the relation of all measurable objects, real or imaginary. I told her I specialized in solving theoretical problems relating to artificial joints. She told me math had never been her strong point, she could never understand the subject. I talked to her about the ancient Greeks, about Thales, Diophantus, and Eratosthenes. She said she had never heard of any of them. I told her of Hypatia and Archimedes. The latter she was familiar with, she said, but it turned out, she was confusing him with Pythagoras. I told her mathematics had been created by God. However, right after that, I added, the devil came along, threw in the alphabet and fucked things up. Fortunately, she laughed. Then she told me she never liked physics either! I said that there, she had a point. She gave me an odd look and remained silent. I explained that physics was a branch of science that makes the simple movement of a billiard ball seem extremely complicated. She laughed. Then we talked about her ex-husband. She told me that despite him being a good-for-nothing liar and a cheat, he was well-built and well-endowed, with an 8-inch cock. Yeah, I said, sure, but did it crow at dawn? She didn't get it and didn't laugh. Things were going great! Then she told me she wanted to lose some weight. I disagreed. She liked that. She said I had a good body and asked if I worked out. I told her the last time I was in a gym, I remember right afterwards, I had detention. She didn't get that either, didn't laugh. Then I told her the only exercise I ever do is chase my daily running expenses. She laughed at that. I asked her when was the last time she had weighed herself. She said she weighed herself every morning. She asked me when *I* had last been weighed and I replied, *In the maternity clinic.* Once again, she didn't laugh. I could understand that. We were doing great! Then she complained she had lots of beauty spots on her back. Actually, she did have a lot of tiny spots. Nothing tragic, though. God knows what some idiot had said to her and made her so self-conscious. I told her to go get a tattoo of a leopard. This time, she burst out into peals of laughter.

Semy and I got along like a house on fire. Both of us knew what we wanted. I wanted sex and she wanted companionship. We each got what we wanted. We were together for six months and eleven days. I was in seventh heaven. We were having a fabulous time. And all the time we were together, there was one thing that had become obvious to me. The secret to not missing sex was to have sex. Well, at some point we finally broke up, very amicably and tearfully, as her aunt had brokered a marriage for her with a 39-year-old Greek restaurateur from Chicago who was loaded, and who she liked very much. For the record, I stated I was a bit upset, but to be perfectly honest, I was devastated.

All the time we were together we never fought. We respected one another and we took care not to cause any stress or create tense situations between us. With Lillian and Fanouris, we didn't socialize as couples outside the house, as Lillian acted snobbish around Semy. She looked down on her for her lack of education, as she hadn't finished high school, and also because she was the cleaning woman at the Greek church. In addition, it annoyed her that Semy didn't have much of a sense of humor, while in my case, though she thought I was amusing, and said I made her laugh, she considered the age difference between us and them to be a big problem. She even told me outright one day that I was old. I tried to set her straight that old can be good at times– like old songs, old movies and best of all, old friends. But she didn't get it. What can I say, that's the way the girl had been brought up. Whenever Semy and I found ourselves in the apartment when Lillian was there, we always kept things civil. Though, as far as I was concerned, I could barely stand the girl. She was pretty for sure, amusing, too, but still a spoilt brat and a self-centered little bitch.

Poor Fanouris. Even though he liked Semy a lot, and considered me his best friend, what could he do? He'd back down. She led him by the nose. In any case, it didn't really matter much that we didn't hang out together. We managed fine without them. Especially without her.

One time, Semy really scared the shit out of me. She announced that her period was late and was afraid she might be pregnant as her diaphragm had slipped out of place. I felt my heart pounding so fast it was as if I were on a highway to Hell. You can't imagine what it meant to get a girl pregnant back in those days in the good old US of A, and especially in the south-central states. Abortions were completely illegal and if they did happen, carried a huge risk, a high rate of accidents and complications as they were carried out by amateur midwives, mostly black women, or by quacks, unqualified foreign doctors, usually illegals without a license to practice, or even medical students, and usually executed on some kitchen table or in a filthy basement under unhygienic conditions, without sterilized surgical instruments. And they cost a fortune, to boot.

I can still recall the day Semy came to me like some poor miserable creature, curled up and snuggled in my arms on the couch where I was sitting watching television and, gazing up at me with her huge green eyes brimming with tears, softly asked me:

If I'm pregnant, what will we do?

Have a baby, I trust, I answered seriously.

What do you mean? she asked and I explained.

I had made my decision and it was unshakeable. From the minute she had told me, I had mulled it over and over in my head. Every which way. Seriously. If she were pregnant, I'd marry her, and we'd keep the child. I'd never expose her to any kind of danger, for whatever reason. She didn't deserve that. I really meant it and I told her so. I remember how she embraced me and burst into tears. I had made her happy. That's what she said to me.

For me, all this turned out for the best. From that day on, she swallowed.

We'd had countless discussions on this subject. She always reacted. Never wanted to. In fact, she once complained that every boyfriend she'd ever had, had asked her the same thing. To swallow. I told her that was the natural thing to do. I explained that the only man who would ever tell her, *'Don't swallow, spit'* is the dentist. No one else. That she got and she howled with laughter. However, pregnant she was not, as she found out a few days later, but she was thrilled and happy with me, because, as she said, I had passed the crash test with great success.

Another matter that bothered her, and she showed it, was that wherever we happened to be, I was always pushing her into having sex. Logical, isn't it? It was something that had been missing from my life in general. Wherever we went, to the movies, for a drive, or at home, I needed it. She didn't always feel like it and we'd argue. Trying to convince her, we'd talk on and on, nonstop. In exasperation, once, I told her the only way for us to shut up about it was if she gave me a blow job; that would definitely shut us both up. She didn't get that.

In general, though, I felt I was just fine with what I had. Happy. However, every Sunday, I did light a huge candle in church, just for good measure.

With the girls at home, whenever we were all together, we spoke in English. Lillian, on the one hand, didn't speak Greek well and made quite a few cute mistakes, while Semy, after so many years in the US, had forgotten some of her Greek and was constantly searching for words, which she couldn't always find, to finish her sentences.

In any event, we joked around a lot with Greek to English transliterations. Once, I remember, we had just come home with Semy from a meal at an Indian restaurant that we had gone to with a group of colleagues from the university. The food had been very good, but for sensitive American stomachs used to bland foods, the chilies and spices used in curries were a bit too much to handle. Semy wasn't feeling so good. We sat down to listen to some music and have a drink and I noticed she seemed a bit queasy. At that moment, Fanouris and Lillian showed up, who had gone to the movies. While we were chatting, Fanouris also noticed Semy didn't look too good. He asked her how she was and she told him the food had upset her. He suggested she go to the bathroom and throw up, so she'd feel better. She replied she couldn't do that because 'vomiting on command' wouldn't work for her. That's when Lillian put in her two cents worth:

Why don't you go use your finger to relieve yourself?

Semy turned to me in surprise and said in Greek:

What did she just say? I only want to throw up, not make myself come!

When the girls saw me and Fanouris in the grips of hysterical laughter, they just stared at us as if we had totally lost it! They couldn't understand what was so funny. Lillian hadn't the faintest idea of what Semy had actually said, and Semy, on the other hand, had no idea one could upchuck by sticking a finger down one's throat.

When all the necessary explanations were given, things returned to normal. Semy used her finger and learned yet another use for it.

On another afternoon, I had phoned Semy at home, like I often did, and for kicks, I tried to phone-sex her.

Tell me, what do you have on? I asked her in Greek.

Right now? She answered, pissing me off.

No, when you go fishing, I told her. She didn't get it.

When I explained what I had been trying to do, she laughed that her answer had annoyed me.

Another image just came to mind. One day the four of us had stayed at home, as the weather had turned foul. It was raining buckets and very cold. We sat around chatting, as usual, with music on in the background. Out of the blue, Fanouris declared how happy he was waking up most mornings lying next to Lillian. Semy gave me a sidelong glance and raised an eyebrow since, so far, we had never spent a whole night together.

I know, I said. *It's really awesome when you wake up and kiss the person who is sleeping beside you. It makes you feel glad you're alive and tingly all over. I remember doing that once, but ever since then, I'm persona non grata on that airline.*

Everybody laughed.

In the beginning, Fanouris and Lillian had sexual problems because, as we found out, Fanouris was very impetuous and impatient, and didn't waste time on foreplay. He was young and it seemed he hadn't been taught right, up there in Kozani! Lillian complained constantly but in vain. At some point, she talked to Semy about it. Naturally, Semy told me everything, thinking, as the oldest of the group, I should intervene. What should I do? I thought about it, wracking my brain to find the right approach. Some kind of example that would clearly convey what I was trying to say. Finally, it came to me. I took them all for a drive on a Sunday afternoon and we went to a theme park not too far away, which had some humongous water slides. It was the end of October, so they were out of commission. We got out of the car and strolled toward the slides.

I said to Fanouris:

Hey, man! Do you think you could go down this slide in your bathing trunks without the water running?

Wha-a-a-at! Are you crazy? Hell no!

Why not?

Because I'll skin my ass along with the rest of me, you idiot. Why do you ask?

Now do you understand why foreplay is necessary before sex? I said.

Howling with laughter, he told me he got it.

After we explained to the girls what we had said, they got it, too! This was the only time I can recall ever being kissed by Lillian.

Another time, Semy and I were home and we were just chatting. She was sitting in the living room and I was in the kitchen. It was early in our relationship and we were still in the ooey-gooey lovey-dovey stage. I remember she was talking about us and I constantly kept interrupting.

Why are you interrupting me? She said. *Let me have my dreams. What do you have?*

Meatballs, I replied.

Giggling, she turned to look at me.

I wasn't kidding. As a matter of fact, I *was* making meatballs. I had bought the ground meat, half beef and half pork, passed through the grinder once only, from the Hungarian butcher at Fanouris' supermarket. To this I added breadcrumbs, onions processed in the blender, finely chopped fresh parsley and dried mint. Then I threw in two egg yolks, a shot of ouzo, egg whites whipped up into a meringue, some virgin olive oil, salt and pepper. After combining everything together and shaping the mixture into meatballs, it was time for my special tweaks, picked up from watching my grandmother when she used to make the most fucking incredible meatballs. First, with wet hands, I roll the meatballs in a crumb mixture, a 50-50 ratio of finely ground rusks and flour. The trick is to bread them twice. For the second time, I sprinkle them with cold water and roll them again in the breadcrumbs. Then, in they go into boiling oil for 4 minutes. That's all there's to it. You can't imagine how melt-in-your-mouth tender these meatballs are. Anyone who's ever had one, still remembers how great they are!

One evening, the four of us had gone out together, a rare occasion for us. We had gone to one of my favorite hangouts, a lovely bar in the center of town, for Semy's birthday. We had drinks and listened to live music by a local little- known youth band. It was nice. The lead singer was a twenty-year-old kid with long hair and shiny silver hip-hugging bell bottoms. He had a great resounding voice, but his pants were so tight one could make out the outline of his dick. Fanouris and I hadn't noticed anything at first, but then we saw the girls snickering and giggling. Especially Lillian, who, every so often would lean over and whisper something in Semy's ear, and then they'd both burst out laughing. At some point, after our constant questioning and badgering, they finally told us what was what! Now it was our turn to crack up. Though, seriously, between you and me, the kid *was* very well-endowed, if what we were seeing was really his, and not some strategically placed sock! Afterwards, as was to be expected, the conversation circled around the question of size, and whether or not this played any particular role in bed. Our discussion became heated. Because we were speaking loudly - to be heard over the music - people at some of the tables around us latched on to our conversation. Things got even livelier, more intense, with various arguments from both sides. Then Lillian, who by now was blushing madly, said she felt embarrassed by this conversation and didn't wish to continue it. Fanouris signaled we should leave. But I was enjoying myself. I wasn't ready to go yet. So I raised my hands and shouted, *Quiet please! Could I have your attention for just a minute?* Immediately conversations died down and several pairs of eyes were trained on me.

So, I said, *I believe size does play a big role in bed, and I'll explain at once exactly what I mean.* I saw that Semy, Lillian, Fanouris and quite a few others were staring intently at me, half-smiling.

The bigger the size of the bed, I continued, *the better, and more comfortably, I sleep. I rest my case.*

Needless to say, after I had finished, all hell broke loose! Loud applause and wolf-whistles could be heard from all corners of the bar. Suddenly, a random bunch of guys came over, laughing boisterously and slapping me on the back, while we were offered a couple more rounds of free drinks. We stayed on at the bar until late.

Generally speaking, we were having a good time with the girls. I don't know about Fanouris, but I was having a blast. Semy wasn't putting any pressure on me. Our relationship was cool and there were never any scenes between us. The change in me was even apparent to the naked eye. My professor and I were working on some non-linear equations one day when he turned to me and asked:

Come on, Dino. Tell us your secret. You seem to have found the fountain of happiness somewhere.

My smile said it all. Words were not necessary.

There was nothing about Semy that was affected. She was uncomplicated and always calm. Always smiling, sweet and good-natured. Whenever anything went awry, she was sure that the Good Lord would take care of it. Her faith was great and profound. There was no arguing about that. Occasionally, I'd take her to a lecture on campus. She'd be bored out of her mind but then I'd take her to a bar or two and we'd have a great time, lots of laughs. She seemed to enjoy academic life - at least, the way I was living it.

Everyone who met her inevitably liked her and appreciated her company. The other Greeks and whoever else dropped in for a bite to eat, always asked about her. She had won them all over. Some called just to find out how she was and what she was up to. I remember once, soon after Semy and I had first met, my friend Panos from Thebes, whom I've told you about, doing his doctorate in chemistry, gave me a call:

Come on, buddy, tell me. How are things coming along with your girl?

Almost finishing.

What? You're breaking up already?

No! We're fucking and I'm about to come. So, hang up.

In any case, Semy eventually got all my Greek friends to end up in church one Sunday morning, where Father Charalambis quickly won them over. They all started attending his services regularly. Fact was, that priest was truly a remarkable fellow. It was as if God Himself had chosen him to head the Orthodox church here. Who knows? Maybe that was actually true.

Suddenly, around March, we lost Elias. Elias was doing a BA in business administration. Fanouris and he had been going to the same catechism classes every Saturday at the church. Elias had hit on a pretty, dark-haired chick there who had told him she was 18. I think her name was Helen. Turns out, she still had two months to go before turning 18. And Elias was in a hurry. Helen was so thrilled she went and bragged to her friends who in turn told others, etc., until word finally reached her home. It turned out that the mother of one of her best friends was Helen's mother's hairdresser.

They said she had been seduced. Her father was a hotshot contractor and was loaded, ready to hire a team of star lawyers to go after him. Elias would've ended up in prison with a ten-year sentence at least.

Helen warned Elias who realized he was up shit's creek. Within two days, he got his nomenclature from the university, shoved everything he had into a couple of suitcases and took off. A lot later, we found out he had fled to an aunt of his in Queens and had enrolled in some university in New York. In any event, the girl's parents were persuaded by Father Charalambis to drop any action against him.

Years later, when Fanouris and I met up again back home in Greece, he told me that Helen had turned into quite an achiever. She had had two quickie marriages that had both ended in divorce, no children, and with money from her dad and a settlement from her first husband, she had opened a big jazz bar in the center of town which had become very fashionable and she was really raking it in. He and Helen even had a thing going for a while. Fanouris told me some of the crazy stuff the two of them had gotten into. Once, he had gone to her bar one evening because Benny Goodman was scheduled to play and he was really into jazz. He was sitting alone at a table having a drink and when Helen spotted him, she went over and joined him. They talked for a while about the good old times. At one point, for fun, he asked her:

How many guys have you actually been with?

Five, she replied.

Are you kidding me? he exclaimed, unbelievingly.

I admit, that was *a weird night.*

That had stunned Fanouris. He told me that after her second divorce, people were saying that she had hooked up with a gorgeous redhead from Idaho, even shacked up with her. Crazy stuff. I remember thinking what a riot all of that was and I burst out laughing! I told him it seemed that Helen was one of those chicks that when you're about to fuck them, and you ask:

How do you like it, on top or on the bottom?

They'd reply:

In the middle.

We both laughed.

In any event, from the time I left the States, I've been back around ten times actually, but never to the place I got my degree from. I'd like to go back sometime before I die. Or maybe in my next life.

Fanouris added that Elias had finally finished college with a degree from NYU, went on for an MA at Columbia and then went back to Greece. He did his military service and then got a job at a bank. He's been active in politics for a while now.

He's an MP for the Pan-Socialist Party, he added.

You're kidding! Is that so? I thought I recognized him. Go figure.

We get together once in a while. Want to join us next time we go out?

Sure! You've got my mobile. It's still the same, hasn't changed.

OK! I'll give you a call.

We ordered a couple more beers and I asked him about Petros who had married Nancy after she got pregnant and quit pharmacology. Fanouris' expression darkened a notch. He told me that Nancy had had a healthy baby girl who choked to death on something when she was two. She and Petros split up seven months after that. They just couldn't handle the tragedy, it really crushed them. Petros eventually got involved in the catering business and became a big success. Pulled in all the business in the territory. Never got married again, never had another kid. But Nancy remarried a couple of years later and had twin boys. That news really shocked me.

I asked Fanouris where Petros was now and if he was still in touch with him.

We stayed in touch until about two years ago, he replied. *Until he died.*

I froze. *What the hell, man? What do you mean, died? What happened?* I was truly stunned.

Found out he had been racing in a brand-new yellow Camaro he had just picked up from the dealership. You remember that flat stretch on Route 35 that passes by the campus and intersects with 240? That's where it happened.

I was speechless. I had always admired Petros. He was great company, and really good-hearted. Great sense of humor; played guitar beautifully and had a great voice. I had always thought, though, he was an unlucky sort. And I wasn't proved wrong, after all. What a pity. I had even gone to his wedding, for crissakes!

Say something, man, Fanouris said. *At a loss for words?*

That was really upsetting, man. Life truly sucks! Like a goddam EKG. A flatline kills, I blurted out, not really realizing what I was saying.

For a while, both of us were silent. Then Fanouris chuckled.

You haven't changed, man. That's why I like you. This was as good a memorial for him as it gets. Well… to life… and may God forgive him! he cried out as our glasses met in a toast.

The night wore on and we talked forever. We didn't skip anyone, I don't think. He told me that now Semy had three kids, two boys and a girl. She had even baptized her second boy at the church there, Saint George. Fanouris had attended, along with the boy's godfather, Sotiris, who was the church's administrator, from Trikala. I can't say I remember him at all.

Fanouris added that with the pregnancy, she had put on some weight she couldn't get rid of. I asked him if he had a chance to speak with her.

Of course, I did, he replied. *And we even kept up a correspondence, first on paper and then online. She asked after you occasionally, wondering what you were up to. She seemed pleased to hear that you were fine. She mentioned that she had often spent summers in Greece with her family. They had even bought a piece of land on Corfu to build a house. Her husband had fallen in love with the island.*

I smiled, recalling what I had said to her once about her hometown Igoumenitsa.

Then suddenly I felt a bit sad, realizing that Semy must be over sixty by now.

Fanouris also told me about Panos, with whom I had lost touch, saying he had done very well for himself. He was living in Michigan, working at Dow Chemical as an executive director in one of their production facilities. He had married – he didn't know to whom – and had three children, now grown up. He had run into him, purely by chance, when he had gone to the States to Lansing, Michigan four years ago on business, something to do with new technologies, internet or some such thing.

I asked Fanouris for his contact info and he gave it to me, along with his email address. I felt I needed to get in touch with Panos.

And there were more names from the past. I learned that Filippos had received his PhD with high honors and had taught biology at Stanford University for several years. He had married a Polish-American girl who was working as a researcher at the university's biology lab. They had three kids, two boys and a girl. For the past several years, he's been a lecturer in biology at Cambridge. Well done! The man deserved it. Very dedicated and active, as I recall. An impressive guy.

Fanouris brought up others as well, some of whom I remembered, others I didn't. For my part, I mentioned that I had run into Manousos who was an ORL at Evangelismos Hospital in Athens. Fanouris wasn't impressed. And didn't ask for details.

I asked him if he had any news about Pam or Phyllis and he told me what he knew. I'll tell you later all about these two.

And when I asked about Father Charalambis, Fanouris told me that he had advanced well up the ladder of the church's hierarchy and had been appointed an archimandrite or something else to that effect. I was pleased to learn that. The man deserved it. The truth is, some people seem to be born to do what they eventually do later in life. He was definitely one of them. He had the gift. All the best to him.

Aside from all the news, I was really glad I had run into Fanouris after all these years and to learn he was doing well. He was now a successful professional, with his own company. And married for many years to Julia, a career officer at Eurobank, with whom he had two beautiful daughters, 18 and 19 years old.

Fanouris and I had lived together for over a year back then. But though he had spent four more years there after I left, he had never gone back either. A pity.

Semy and I split up in early May. Truth be told, I had sensed that something wasn't quite right earlier, but I hadn't given it much thought. You'll say, 'Well, you should have.' But it wasn't like that. Let me explain. I had my priorities. I was totally dedicated to what I was doing. And I was approaching the end. I could touch it. I could see that my mathematical models were working. I was on the right path.

The world of mathematics is magical. It's so easy to get lost in it. It's like living in a Brothers Grimm fairy tale. You're waiting for Snow White, the Big Bad Wolf or the bewitched Prince to leap out of the pages – or the math equations you're solving. It takes a lot of attention and self-discipline not to be carried away. Slow, careful steps. You often have to retrace. You're seeking the truth, after all. And when you can finally fall upon a proof that's been tormenting you, eluding you for so long, the satisfaction you feel is indescribable. As if you've scored the most beautiful woman in the world. As if you've vanquished an entire army, an evil dragon. Your heart pounds and you can almost feel the blood coursing through your veins. Your temples feel as if they're about to burst. I had solved the problem I had been assigned. I forced myself to calm down and then, as ruthlessly as I could, I went over everything, inch by inch. I scoured it all, equation by equation, point by point, looking for a flaw. Not finding anything, I took my work to my professor. Coolly, he took the thick file and, without even looking through it, he put it in a drawer. He told me to go home and take it easy. A few days later, I learned that he had passed it on to a committee of three colleagues to go over it - standard procedure. I was aware that this was how it was done – my professor wouldn't even look at it until the committee passed it back to him. I didn't expect to receive a verdict, positive or negative, for at least a couple of weeks. If I had made a mistake somewhere, at best, I would go back and try to resolve it. I knew this because it had already happened to me before. If it was sound, my professor would hand the file back to me, instructing me to publish. Publish! The magic word every single post-graduate student craves to hear. It meant it was all finally over. The process of publishing which included preparing the bibliography took anywhere from one month to four. Only a month if you happened to be a reincarnation of Gauss or Riemann, but up to four months if you were of humbler mathematical stock. If all went well, for me, it was more likely to take up to four months.

I say all this to show you what my state of mind was at that time. I really had no time for anything else. Not for Semy, not for my mom who grumbled on the phone that I never gave any sign of life anymore, not for anyone nor anything. Christ, it's like you're captain of a ship with only your map and the only working instrument a compass, forging ahead in the dead of night through savage stormy seas in the middle of nowhere, hoping to reach the port you're aiming for. Your attention is riveted on the island ahead. You're looking for some indication you're on the right course, that you haven't strayed. You know that there are reefs, jagged rocks everywhere, ready to tear you apart. You can't think of food, of drink, not even of pissing or of sleeping. You're trapped there, holding the wheel tightly, your knuckles white with the strength of your grip, the wind shrieking and howling around the cabin, waves battering the craft, water furiously forcing its way through any gaps in the bulkheads – while your eyes peer into the darkness, seeking out something, anything in that blackness. Imagine then how you'd feel if in that maelstrom you finally discern a light. Faint. You head in that direction, your heart pounding away mercilessly inside you, hoping that it's what you seek. And the closer you draw near, and you realize that it's the harbor you were aiming for, the crazier you get. So easy now to missteer, make a mistake and sacrifice everything. This ordeal of bringing the ship safely to port through the maelstrom had taken me around 40 days. Through all that time, I was in another world. After handing in my work, I went back home and threw up. All my pent-up exhaustion just poured out of me. I don't know how many hours I slept. I remember, though, that I was awakened by the persistent ringing of the phone. I got up, zombie-like, and grabbed hold of the receiver. It was Semy. She was glad she finally found me, she said. She wanted to see me, to talk. Urgently. I got worried. I looked at my watch. It was 8. I didn't know if it was night or day. God knows how I managed to speak or what I said but I heard her say:

Let it be. I'll come over.

And, in fact, a half hour later, she showed up. I had barely managed to have a shower, shave and put on the sweat suit I normally wore around the flat.

She used her key to enter and came over and kissed me. She went into the kitchen to make coffee. She called out, asking if I wanted any and I said I did. A few minutes later, she came into the living room with two mugs and sat down on the sofa opposite me. She looked at me and told me to spit it out, verbatim.

I laughed and began to explain what I had been up to all the time I hadn't been in touch. I had been camping out at the library, spending little time at my office on campus. I'd just pop over to the apartment every few days for a bath and a shave. I broke every record in the book. I had barely slept a wink for ten days straight. The last few days, I had been able to catch a few hours' sleep a day in the armchair in my office. I told Semy everything, talking for almost an hour. She didn't interrupt me at all.

Then she took over. She spoke of her life, telling me stuff I more or less already knew. She talked about her parents, about how she had felt when she had lost them. She spoke about her lousy marriage; she felt betrayed because she had been raised with the belief that marriage was a sacred institution, with her parents as her model. That notion had been laid bare. She spoke of how much she had wanted to have a baby but added that she was so relieved that it hadn't happened. The child would have been raised without a dad.

Then she segued into our relationship, how it had evolved over the last several months and what it had come to. That's when she paused.

Now, please tell me what the future holds for us, she said.

She had caught me unprepared. I commented that I had entered into the relationship for some human companionship.

She smiled. *You mean, for the sex. Isn't that so?*

I replied that she was right but that it had gone beyond that. I felt an enormous tenderness for her, maybe even love, I wasn't sure. But I knew that she meant a lot to me.

She smiled again, with that beautiful smile of hers. *Had the thought of marrying ever crossed your mind?*

She had me cornered. I had never imagined that I would have been the subject of a marriage proposal from a woman. I responded by saying that at that time, no, but the way our relationship had progressed, it was very possible in the future.

She looked straight at me and asked, *And what kind of time frame do you have in mind when you say, 'in the future'?*

I explained that I saw two courses: the first was I would leave the States after receiving my degree and return to Greece. I'd ask her to follow me shortly after, when I had found a decent job with good prospects, as long as she felt she needed to be with me. The other course was to work on funded government research programs here at the university. As a researcher, I would get a green card right away. In that case, our relationship would evolve as it had been evolving.

I stopped and looked at her.

For a moment, we were both silent.

Then she spoke. *Unfortunately, all that is a little too vague for me. I don't grasp the extent of your commitment.*

Of course, she was absolutely right. I didn't know how to respond. She had blindsided me with this talk. What the hell? What had brought this on? Had something happened?

That's when she told me about the restaurateur from Chicago. Her aunt had brought him over to her place for her to meet him. At first, she wasn't interested. She had tried to get in touch with me time and time again but with no luck. She had even called in the middle of the night several times. She had called Fanouris, too, waking him up from a deep sleep to ask him where I was. He had no idea where I was or what I was doing. She tried calling Lillian as well, but she couldn't tell her anything either. She had tried calling me at my office on campus, with no luck. It was if the earth had swallowed me whole. She didn't know what to do. All she had wanted was for me to put my arms around her and hold onto what we had. But she couldn't find me anywhere. She had needed to draw strength from our bond, but I was not there. In the meantime, her aunt was pressuring her. She had even enlisted Father Charalambis's help and he was pressuring her as well. Finally, to get them off her back, she agreed to go out with this guy from Chicago. And as it turned out, she liked him. He was a nice guy - serious, hard-working, and straight as an arrow. She made it clear that honesty was what most important to her, given her grim experience with her ex-husband. That bastard had left her with an open wound in that respect. She added that this man had said he wanted to get married right away and leave for Chicago, where he had his successful business and a large house.

I didn't know what to say. I stared at her, speechless.

You realize that my biological clock is ticking faster than yours. I have to decide about my future before it's too late, she commented.

All I could do was stare. I don't know what was showing on my face, but she smiled. She reached over to me and caressed my cheek.

I'm sorry about all this. I realize I caught you by surprise, isn't that right?

When do you leave for Chicago? I stammered.

Soon, she replied.

I realized I was losing her, and that it was final. I could feel the blood rushing to my head. Suddenly, I didn't want to lose her.

I'll stay! I'll go talk to my professor tomorrow, I said, desperate.

No! You're not going anywhere. No sudden decisions in the heat of the moment that might risk your future because of me. It isn't what you really want. If you did want it, you would have done so already.

Dammit, she was right. But that didn't stop me from coming up with all kinds of protestations.

She put her hand over my mouth. *Just shut up and come closer and hold me.*

I put my arms around her and held her tightly. She smelled warm and wonderful. She held me lightly, one hand caressing my hair, the other slowly running up and down my back.

I really do love you, she whispered into my ear. *You were the best thing that could have happened to me at this stage of my life. You really were. I'll always remember you fondly. I mean it.*

I felt that I had a lot to say myself, but nothing seemed to be coming out. I was all choked up. All I could manage was a weak sob, my eyes filling with tears. She moved back a little and looked into my eyes. She kissed away a tear that was sliding down my cheek. Then she placed her lips softly, very softly, on mine, and closed her eyes. We kissed for a long time.

It was the first time we spent the entire night together. My sleep was restless. Every time I was awakened by some shitty dream or other and looked at her in the dim glow from the streetlight outside the window, I saw her lying on her side, supporting her head on her hand, her lovely green eyes open, looking at me. She would smile and then caress my hair gently until I fell asleep again for a while. That lasted until 4 in the morning. Then I fell into a deep sleep from which I didn't wake up until 8. I sat up and looked around me. She wasn't there. She had left.

She had even taken her toothbrush. All she left behind of herself was the photo in its frame on my desk. I found her set of keys on the kitchen counter. I never saw her again. I passed by the church but she wasn't there. Another girl had taken her place. With a smile, Father Charalambis told me she had quit to make a change in her life. He advised me not to go looking for her at her place. It would only end badly. Of course, he knew all about us. The whole world knew everything and there we were, trying to keep it a secret.

Needless to say, I drove past her place a few times, but didn't see any sign of life. No surprise, since her car was gone as well. I went back home, had a bath and then left for my class. That afternoon, since I didn't have any more classes until I received the verdict on my thesis from the university, I went out, bought myself a bottle of Four Roses bourbon, returned home, downed the whole thing and passed out. When Fanouris came back from his job at the supermarket, he found me sprawled out on the couch, totally wasted, the empty bottle lying on the floor. He brought over a blanket, covered me, turned off the stereo, switched the lights off and went to bed.

After Semy, my life changed.

At first, I had no appetite for going out. I'd just stay at home, slumped on the couch in front of the TV, smoking a lot, bemoaning my fate, the stereo blaring, drinking whatever I could find in the house, eating sandwiches and sleeping. At most, whenever I felt like it, I'd pick up the phone if it rang, but that was about it. Didn't even go to church.

All I did was go to my classes. Probably better if I hadn't. I was an obvious mess. Unshaven, unkempt, my clothing wrinkled, shoes unpolished, eyes red. I could see that my students were alarmed. The dean called me in eventually and asked me what was going on. I didn't know what to say. All that came to mind was to say that my father had died. Which wasn't untrue. It was just that I was four years old when he had died. The dean warmly offered his condolences and told me take the rest of the week off.

The news travelled fast throughout the school, even reaching the church. Fanouris told me Sunday afternoon that everyone was asking after me, telling him to offer me their condolences and best wishes. As for Father Charalambis, he didn't say a word; all he did was smile at Fanouris conspiratorially. The next day, I was expecting to go back to my teaching job at noon, marking the tenth day that I had been acting like some kind of zombie. But around nine-thirty that morning, the phone rang. I was informed that I was to report to my professor at eleven. I took a bath, shaved, dressed, pulled myself together, put on a tie, slapped a smile on my face and left the house, feeling anxious.

My professor opened the door himself, greeting me with a beaming smile. He asked me to sit down opposite him. On his desk, I spotted the file with my notes, plus a few typewritten sheets. I could feel my heart throbbing in my ears.

He began by saying that my work was very good, and he liked it. That was what more or less every mathematician he had given it to for review had said as well, according to the reports he had on his desk. He made a few observations regarding my presentation. That I should add a few references or develop further proofs of certain theorems. He continued , but I was no longer listening. My mind was afire, anxious to hear the magic words. Finally, he stood up, picked up the file from his desk and handed it to me, saying, *You may type and submit it.*

Yes! That was it! The culmination of all my efforts. I had succeeded, but I suddenly felt the enormity of the cost: my efforts had cost me Semy. I almost stood up and kissed him. I held back, though. I thanked him profusely for his help and guidance. He protested that he hadn't done anything, my success was entirely due to own my efforts. All he did was to make sure I stayed on track. Which was, in fact, a considerable contribution. He added that we had to get together the following week to go over the material prior to publishing.

I almost flew out of his office. I went to my class. The difference in my appearance was dramatic. Mrs. Lee asked me what had happened and I told her. She congratulated me and later, when I went to gather my things from the professors' lounge to leave, everyone was there, greeting me with applause and a bottle of red wine. A wonderful feeling. I admit I was thrilled.

I had plenty of time ahead of me to write up my final paper for publishing. In those days, there were no PCs with a printer attached to make things easy. We typewrote the text, added the mathematical symbols in ink by hand and corrected mistakes with white-out before photocopying each page. That was an improvement. At the beginning of our college years, we had to prepare stencils and mimeograph our work. Tragic circumstances!

Feeling great, that afternoon, I cooked. I made an eggplant with filet mignon dish with a side of boiled zucchini. Plus, I put together a nice, fresh salad with various types of lettuce, arugula, little plum tomatoes, strips of cucumber and gruyère shavings.

I sliced the eggplant in thick rounds, generously applied salt and pepper and arranged them on a greased baking sheet. I sprinkled with olive oil and roasted them in a hot oven until they browned (30 min).

In a colander, I sliced the tomatoes thickly, sprinkled them with a bit of salt and let them drain. I arranged them on another baking pan, added some ground pepper, crushed garlic, a bit of basil and sprinkled with olive oil I roasted them in the hot oven for around 30 min as well.

In the meantime, I cut the filet into medium-sized slices which I then grilled lightly on both sides. Then I assembled my ingredients: one layer of eggplant, one of filet, another of eggplant, then tomato, and topped with grated cheese. I sprinkled paprika on them and roasted them for 15 minutes. They turned out great. I served them with the salad I had made, to which I added a few thinly-sliced mushrooms and a vinaigrette with lots of vinegar. When Fanouris came home at a quarter past five as he did every day, he went wild. So did Lillian who arrived a little later. Fanouris phoned Panos and told him to get his ass over and come taste something he had never had before. And told him if he did come, to bring some bread. Panos showed up a short while later, a loaf of bread under his arm. We sat around the table and had a whale of a time.

Around seven that evening, I took Fanouris, Lillian, Panos and his girlfriend, Lucy, who was finishing up in biology, and we went out for a drink to celebrate my success. Fanouris planned to leave us before eight to get to his job at the supermarket.

It was obvious to everyone though, despite the occasion, that I was feeling Semy's absence. I found my attention wandering, not listening to what they were saying. I forced a laugh whenever they laughed but it was apparent my mind was elsewhere. What I wanted to hear was her sweet and tender voice and I wasn't hearing it. I missed her. I was beginning to feel angry and I didn't know why.

Fanouris and Lillian whispered between them for a few moments. A few moments later, as Fanouris and I were heading for the men's room, he told me that they were going to introduce me to a cousin of Lillian's. Later, when the girls went to the ladies' room, Panos mentioned that Lucy had a friend who had just broken up with her boyfriend and they were going to introduce her to me. I said, fine. What else could I say? Imagine if I ended up not knowing which one to choose. But at that moment, I didn't want anyone. I felt that I'd lost all faith in women. I felt rejected. I knew that they weren't at all to blame, but that's how I felt. I realized that what I was feeling wasn't right, but that's what was going on in my head. Semy's flight had done me a lot of damage. I had never imagined I could feel so bad.

The only female I could ever trust again was a delicious tart. So I decided I'd slap one together the very next day. I ordered another bourbon to numb my brain. My fourth. I'd leave my car behind and get Panos or someone else to drive me or I'd take a cab. Fine. That made me feel better. I downed the drink in one gulp and ordered another.

Hold your horses, man, I heard someone say. I looked up and saw that Cretan fellow, Manousos, smiling at me. He was leaning over Panos, his arm around his shoulder. He told us he had arrived a few minutes earlier and was sitting with some of his fellow doctors a few tables away. He had spotted me and seen that I had been downing my drinks one after another with a frequency he found alarming.

We didn't hang out with Manousos very much. I didn't care for him really because he didn't like spaghetti with meat sauce. I found this totally unacceptable, being by my very nature a devout believer in spaghetti Bolognese. I also had a particular soft spot for *pastitsio*, that unparalleled casserole consisting of layers of macaroni, meat sauce, cheese and béchamel. Anyway, even though he was about to graduate from med school, I found Manousos to be rather uncultured and somewhat uncouth.

Fanouris had cautioned me to not provoke him because he was from Crete. What did that mean? I didn't get it. What was the problem with Cretans? My friend Yiannis, born in the US of a Cretan mother and father, studying aircraft design, was Cretan, and he was super guy. A real ace.

In any event, except for the fact that Manousos and I exchanged hellos at the cafeteria occasionally and he had even come over to my place for dinner a couple of times, we really didn't hang out together. I do remember that he had mentioned to me once that the human skeleton consisted of 206 bones, and I had replied that I found that bit of trivia 'mind-blowing'. This, over a few drinks.

Panos told him that I had just gotten the go-ahead to publish. Manousos slapped me on the back and said, *Congrats!* He asked about Semy. From the corner of my eye, I noticed Fanouris gesturing but before anyone could say anything, I simply replied that we weren't together any longer. Manousos said, *That's a shame.* Then he just said, *See you,* and left. When he had gone, I told the others that they didn't have to protect me as if I were damaged goods. It wasn't the end of the world. Happens all the time.

What can you do? We survive. It's not the worst thing that can happen, after all, is it?

Avoiding looking me in the eye, they all murmured apologies, barely audible over the general chaos of music and conversation in the bar.

I spent the next few days in the library, polishing up my bibliography. The afternoons, I spent in the kitchen, cooking, since that was what relaxed me. June was just a couple of days away and we were beginning to feel the heat. The girls were shedding the extra garments of winter. They had begun to circulate bare-armed, and their bras had been retired to their dresser drawers. The mini made its long-awaited reappearance. And, as we've said, America knows no measure. Accordingly, when I say mini, I mean 3-4 fingers below the crotch.

Needless to say, I was lucky that I had more or less finished my work because I wasn't about to lift a pencil again until September when the cold re-emerged and the girls began to pile on the clothing. It was nice. We'd sit outside the bars, bottles of beer in hand, commenting on the passers-by. Fanouris had started to grumble a lot because exam time was fast approaching – June 14 – and the last seven months he had pretty much abandoned his studies, spending all his time with Lillian. I got hold of him one evening and warned him to crack open a book if he intended to finish the year. That maybe he should hang out with Lillian only once a week for a while. I offered to help him with his courses which were math-heavy such as quantum mechanics and applied mathematics. I suggested he give up his job at the supermarket a week before the exams. He promised he'd do that.

Lillian seemed disappointed when Fanouris told her what we had agreed to. She got over it when he told her it was only for a little while. She'd just have to be patient for a few weeks. On only point was she adamant: that they hang out together twice a week, not just once. It was agreed that she'd drive over to the house in her mother's car as she had just gotten her license.

It looked as if things would proceed smoothly. It was up to Fanouris now and the effort he put into it to make it work. After we arranged all this, in the evening, we all went out. Lillian also brought Miriam along.

Miriam was a cousin on her mother's side. She didn't speak a word of Greek. And had no connection with Greece at all. Her father was a lawyer and mother, a nurse. She was 22, had majored in accounting at one of the nearby colleges and was working at the local First National Bank. As far as looks were concerned, she wasn't anything special - a bit horsey. A large, long face with big teeth. But she was super tall. She was a good one or two inches taller than me, without heels – hers, I mean. One could say she was cute, but beautiful? No way! But wow, was she built! Couldn't deny that! Pretty slender and nicely toned. She had the longest and most beautiful legs I had ever seen. And her tits? Large and firm, looking skyward. Tough to tear your eyes away. Her ass was firm – totally unpinchable (as I found out later). She was a blond, with straight hair, cut short. Her eyes were a cornflower blue and round. Her gaze was intense but a bit stupefied, like a cow's. But what I liked most about her was her *brio*. She had a spontaneous, explosive personality. And she liked me. That's what Lillian said the next day when she called to tell me.

That afternoon, I gave Fanouris a few difficult math problems to solve and went out looking for her. I ran into her as she was coming out of the bank with some co-workers at five. I honked and she walked over to the car. I invited her to go out for a drink that night and she agreed. We went to my favorite hangout. When we walked in, the barman, Mike, looked at me with an amazed expression.

Wow! Who's this? he asked when he saw us.

A friend, I replied.

What does she do?

She hangs curtains, I said.

He laughed and asked, *The usual?* I said yes. Miriam ordered a Tequila Sunrise. Drinks in hand, we went and sat at a table. In the course of our conversation, I found out she was divorced. She'd married her boyfriend in school and got divorced four months later. I asked her why she dumped him; she replied that he was an asshole. She didn't say anything else about how she found that out all of a sudden. I didn't insist. I asked her where he was now. All she said was, *Somewhere else.* I dropped the subject. Later, she told me she was seeing this guy from her office but didn't feel that it was going anywhere.

The topic of conversation turned toward me. She seemed to know a lot about me. Shit! Was I that famous? I went up to the bar and got us refills. The background music was picking up some steam. Songs by the Doors, mainly. Elvis, T-Rex, Otis Redding, Aretha Franklin, Johnny Cash, Ray Charles, as well as the Rolling Stones and the Beatles followed one after the other. Spirits were heating up. The Yardbird's *For Your Love* was playing. Miriam suddenly flung off her shoes, climbed onto the table and started dancing. And she wasn't the only one. Several other girls were doing the same. But Miriam stood out: she was taller than the others, and she was definitely the hottest. A guy around 30, a bit soused, staggered toward our table, drink in hand and said:

Talk about good, strong legs!

You think? she replied with a grin.

Oh, yeah! he yelled. *Any other table legs would have collapsed by now!*

Pissed, she yelled, *Fuck you!* The guy left with a snigger.

She looked at me. I smiled back at her. She climbed down and said, *Let's go.*

All I said was, *Your place or mine?* and she said mine. I paid and we left.

We had a good time, but at midnight, I had to get dressed and take her home. That killed me, I was really out of it by then.

Fanouris was still studying when I got back. He had managed to solve three of the problems I had given him. He hadn't made it yet to the fourth. I showed him how to solve it and then hit the sack.

Miriam and I got together a few more times after that. Five, maybe six. We had a good time, lots of sex. She dumped me suddenly when the guy from the bank she had been going out with proposed to her. She accepted. I was cool with that.

Fanouris and I spent the rest of the week studying. Basically, I was typing in the living room while he was cracking the books in his room. He needed the quiet while I had to have some music on playing softly in the background. My way of relaxing. Whenever he needed help, he'd call out and I'd go. I had never seen him so dedicated. I was impressed. He was probably not getting more than three or four hours of sleep a night. All he would eat was macaroni and cheese, fried eggs and bacon or a ham, cheese, lettuce and tomato sandwich on white bread, and a Coke. That was it. Nothing else. Not to leave him on his own, I ate the same. But I washed mine down with beer.

At one point during that time, Panos gave me a call to tell me he wanted me to meet that friend of Lucy's he had mentioned, Sandra. She had just gotten a divorce and looking for company. We arranged to meet at

Mike's. He brought Lucy and Sandra with him. Sandra was huge. Like a mountain. Very voluminous. Like a kiosk. Tall and kind of awkward, she did have a very pretty face. I looked at Panos in a panic. *This girl's a mess, you asshole*, I said in Greek. He just grinned and didn't say a word.

Sandra, it turned out, was a social worker in Welfare. She must have held a decent position but, as a woman, she wasn't my type. After a while, pretending I wasn't feeling very well, I made my apologies and high-tailed it out of there.

By the end of the week, I had had it with being cooped up and decided to go out. I called Panos and we agreed to meet at Mike's, since he liked the place too. He showed up without Lucy. Just as well. We talked briefly about the date with Sandra. He told me it had hurt her that I had left so suddenly that day. I responded by saying that if I had stayed any longer, I would have been the one who would have been 'hurt' even more. I asked him if he would have ever gone out with her. He answered, *Where to?* He must have been kidding me. I said that there are statistics that show that fat women outlive guys that tell them they're fat. He laughed.

We moved on, talking about various things, mostly about the future. He mentioned that he had received a few job offers. He was wrapping up his PhD on derivatives of silicon, gallium and arsenic. He explained in detail, and with specific examples, that it was the way of the future. I believed him because I held him in high regard and considered him a rising star. In any event, it turned out that he remained there permanently. He never returned to Greece. He just didn't want to. When I asked him why once, he replied that though he loved Greece, Greece wasn't good for him. I asked about his military service obligation and he said that at some point he would have to go back to serve for a few months at the most as an instructor. I asked how he had come up with this idea and he replied that it would soon be possible because that's how it was being done in other Mediterranean countries – Italy, Spain and France. I nodded. Ri-i-ght! He was really in the dark! This was Greece we were talking about!

I told him so. *And when do you intend to do that, you jerk? When you've landed a solid job, in a highly-competitive field, with obligations, a mortgage on a house, a wife, maybe some kids? What about your parents? Will you ever see them again ? What if something happens to them? What about your brother's wedding? How will you get back into Greece since you'll be classified as a deserter? You know what that means, with the Junta and the colonels running the show there now. What will you have gained? A great job for which you've sacrificed so much, sacrificed everything.*

Great jobs will always be waiting for you, here or anywhere you want to go because you're a star, don't you realize that? Everyone will want you. If you don't know that, I'm sorry, but you're a total asshole.

He looked at me stupidly. I guess he hadn't thought about all that, carried away as he was by his success and all the fabulous job offers he was getting. Matter of fact, some of these offers were accompanied by air tickets to travel to the head offices for an interview, all expenses paid, for three days. And we're talking about the lap of luxury.

OK. I'll see what I'll do. Maybe I'll go in November and get my student exemption extended. It's expiring next year in February. I'll talk to my parents and I'll see. I don't want any hassles.

Right! Then maybe you should just stick to comedy, my friend, I replied.

At that moment, a group of five girls and three guys came into the bar. One of the guys was Jesus, my Mexican friend who had wolfed down half my *pastitsio* once. Remember him? That's the guy. Murat-Erke was with him. He was that blue-eyed, light-haired Turkish friend of mine who came from Smyrna, a civil engineer doing post-graduate work. Going for a PhD in harbour construction. The third guy I had seen before but never met. Our jaws dropped; all five girls were knockouts, one more beautiful than the other. Especially hot were the green-eyed redhead and the blue-eyed blonde. I waved at them to draw the guys' attention. Murat was the first to notice me. He turned and said something to Jesus who looked in our direction and acknowledged us. They sat down at one of the larger tables in the back. Jesus came over soon after. He clapped me on the back and congratulated me, aware I had been given the go-ahead to publish. He, on the other hand, had a ways to go because his subject was a particularly tough problem in topology. He greeted Panos as he knew him as well. I asked him what the story was with the five girls. He laughed and told us they were fourth-year med students. He said that one of them was with Murat, which was obvious from the way they were acting with one another. One of the brunette goddesses was with Xavier, a friend of Jesus from Mexico, the third guy in the group, who was a med student as well. The over six foot tall beauty was with Jesus.

You mean the redhead is on her own? What's her name? I asked him.

She's got a jealous boyfriend, so watch it, he replied.

Come on! What kind of name is that? She some kind of Native American? I asked with a straight face.

He almost pissed himself laughing. Panos, too. Jesus got up and walked back to his table, still laughing. He must have told the others to explain why he was laughing because they all turned to look at us, laughing also.

Panos and I resumed our conversation as the DJ cued in the Doors' *Light my Fire*. Suddenly I felt a tap on my shoulder. I turned to look. It was the tall redhead, the beauty with the green eyes. I was flabbergasted. She stuck her hand out and said, *Hi! I'm She's-Got-A-Jealous-Boyfriend.*

I shook her hand and replied, *I know.*

I asked her to sit down with us and she said, *Why not?* She sat down next to me. I was in a bit of a state. She looked like Rita Hayworth – in her prime! My heart was doing cartwheels. We introduced ourselves. Her name was Phyllis. She was from the next state over. Family of doctors. Father, mother and three older brothers. All doctors.

I said that I heard she was a med student. She told me that was right. I asked her if she could help me. She looked at me curiously and asked me what the matter was. I told her I was in the final stages of despair because I had fallen in love with her the moment I had laid eyes on her.

She laughed. She had the most scintillating laughter I had ever heard. I ordered her a drink. A Manhattan. Our drinks came and we just sat there quietly for a few minutes, enjoying them. I was staring at her. She smiled at me with a quizzical expression.

I said, *You've got incredible eyes.*

Thanks, she replied, smiling, self-assuredly.

Your boyfriend's not coming?

No. Tonight, I'm on my own. Right away, I felt better.

After a slight pause, I said, *You've also got great tits.*

Laughing, she gave me a shove and replied, *You're such a jerk!*

A while later, she said, *They told me you've finished your school. Is that so?*

Not yet, I replied. *I still have to do the stairs. Then I'll be finished.*

We burst out laughing, Panos joining in.

Suddenly, we noticed the blonde, the other Amazon out of the five, coming toward us, the one who looked like Kim Novak, only better. She bent down and whispered something into Phyllis' ear who looked up at her and replied, *I don't care.*

The blonde looked at us and I invited her to join us. Grinning, she shrugged and sat down between me and Panos. In Greek, I said to Panos that he had it made, and he laughed. The girls wanted to know what I had said, and in what language. I said I couldn't tell them because if I did, I'd have to kill them both.

The blonde introduced herself. Her name was Pamela. 'My girl' called her Pam. It suited her. She was remarkably pretty, with short hair, beautiful lips and a fabulous smile. She had blue almond-shaped eyes. Her gaze was piercing.

Her nose was straight, the tip upturned a bit. Her eyebrows were 'chiselled', as my grandmother used to say.

I leaned toward her and whispered in ear, *I could tell from your name. You must be great in bed.*

She choked because, at that moment, she was taking a sip of her drink. She had a coughing fit, spattering her dress. I suggested she come over to my place which was nearby so she could take it off and clean up. She refused but did so with a lot of laughter. Phyllis asked what was so funny. I waited for Pam to give me up but she didn't tell her anything. A good sign.

The tempo of the music had picked up. Rolling Stones, *Satisfaction,* got things kicking. Phyllis was leaning against me, her body moving, and I was beginning to feel the heat. I was sweating.

I put my arm around her shoulders and caressed her earlobe with my thumb. She jerked as if an electric current had passed through her. She shook her head to pull away. Not a good sign.

I asked her if she wanted me to remove my hand. She said no, as long as I didn't move it. I told her I couldn't help it; it was a visceral reaction. She laughed. I asked her if she was into me. She replied that she was already in a relationship.

If I wasn't, she said, *Maybe. In any event I think you're a really interesting guy.*

Thanks for nothing. What was I to do with that?

Then I said, *Can I ask you something? But you've got to answer truthfully.*

Sure. Ask.

Look, I'm only asking this because you're a doctor. Okay?

Come on and get on with it! Ask already!

If a snake bites my dick, will you suck the poison out, so I won't die?

She frowned, even went to get up. I pulled my legs out of the way so she could pass. But she didn't leave. She sat down again. I was laughing. The music had gotten louder. The Animal's *House of the Rising Sun* had just ended and Ray Charles singing *Hit the Road, Jack* had just been cued in. Pam had stopped talking to Panos. She turned and looked at us, first at me, then at Phyllis, and asked what the matter was. I shrugged. Phyllis motioned to her not to say anything.

Pam had been talking to Panos about men's lousy attention span, saying that few men, if any, could concentrate on more than one thing at a time. Women on the other hand, did have that capacity.

She turned to me and asked, *What do you think? Am I right?*

No way! I replied.

She was taken aback. *What do you mean?*

Because I can easily concentrate on your tits even though there are two of them.

She went to say something but instead, suddenly burst out laughing, looking at me strangely. Panos and then Phyllis both joined in the laughter.

I added that there are some very glaring injustices in life perpetrated on the male sex. She looked at me with a dubious yet interested expression.

Explain yourself. What exactly do you mean?

Well, take this cold spell, for instance. The cold makes your nipples hard, but all it does for us is shrink our cocks. A terrible injustice.

She burst out laughing.

I turned to Phyllis. *Don't you agree? Aren't I right?*

Looking straight into my eyes she said, *Whoa, boy! You're getting ahead of yourself...*

I thought of replying that time was running out for me since the academic year was ending soon and I would be leaving, but I said nothing. Instead, a few minutes later, I asked for their phone numbers. They complied. Turned out they had the same number. They were living in the same women's housing facility, the ΑΦΜ sorority. Panos and I gave them our numbers and I got up to leave.

They seemed surprised at that. I said that there were too many things I couldn't get. They asked me what I meant. I said, *When I make a quick move, I'm accused of moving too fast. When I make my move at a casual pace, I'm told I move too slow. And when I play it real cool, they say I'm not interested. So I'm going to go home and get some sleep. Bye to you all.*

Pam grabbed me by the hand and told me not to go. I felt her fingernails lightly run across my palm. It gave me the shivers. I sat down and motioned to Mike to bring us another round. Aretha Franklin was singing *Respect*. I looked at Phyllis. She was smiling. She leaned close to me and, with her eyes half-closed, her pretty nose crinkled, she said, *You're very clever.*

I didn't respond. Pam leaned over and said, *She likes you, can't you see that? Say something sweet to her. She's a very romantic sort, you know.*

I'm not very good at all that, I said.

So, what are you good at?

Mathematics.

She burst out laughing. Phyllis, who had been following what we were saying, joined in.

I turned to Pam. *Can I ask you something?*

She didn't respond but indicated her interest.

Do you cry out when you're having sex? I asked.

No, she replied.

Phyllis, who had been following this, too, smiled.

I turned to her and asked her point blank. *What about you?*

Why do you ask? What's it to you?

I'd like to know.

Why's that?

Let me explain, I said. *If you do cry out, then cry out for me to come over once in a while. Get it?*

They all burst out laughing.

Do you cry out, too? she asked, smiling.

Of course, I do.

And what do you say?

OH, MY GOD! THANK YOU! I replied.

I don't have to tell you how that went down. Suffice it to say, they laughed so hard, everyone in the bar turned to see what was going on at our table.

So the evening went, with lots of trivial conversation and drinking. We completely lost all track of time. We had lots of drinks. After I signalled Mike for another round, I said, *Gone are the days when girls used to cook like their mothers. Now they just drink like their fathers.*

The girls wanted to know if I had a problem with that.

On the contrary, I replied. *I always appreciate girls who can hold their liquor.* That put a stop to any further discussion on that subject.

Eventually, Panos, in Greek, said he was beginning to nod off. I was a little pissed at that, but I told him to leave me 20 bucks and go. He muttered some excuses and sped off after slipping a couple of bills into my pocket. I was left on my own, Odysseus amongst the Sirens. I revelled in it. It was the best thing that could have happened to me and it was happening right now. To the accompaniment of the Archies' *Sugar, Honey, Honey.*

The girls were aching to know what language Panos and I were speaking. That of Homer, I told them. Blank expression. Then I tried them all: Socrates, Plato, Aristotle. Nothing. Spiro Agnew, I tried at last.

That worked. *Greek!* they both cried out at the same time. Wow! Thorough education. They gazed at me in awe. Then they asked me if I was Greek. What could I do? My secret was out, and I was forced to confess.

There followed an endless flow of stupid questions. For instance, where had I learned such good English. So, I told them if they thought they spoke such good English, they were sadly mistaken. They didn't like that. Pam asked if I had ever been to Santorini. I said, not yet. How about Mykonos? Again, no, I hadn't, disappointing them. Then they began to tell me what little they knew about Greece. Pam had more to say because she had been to Athens and Crete with her parents when she was a kid. She remembered the Acropolis and Plaka.

They asked why Plaka was called that. I told them it was because anyone who went in by car and asked someone where to park, the reply was invariably, *You joking, man? You really expect to park here?* They laughed when I told them that 'plaka' was also the Greek word for 'joke'.

It was almost midnight. I asked them if they wanted to come over to my place to listen to some music, have another drink. They looked at each other.

Then Pam turned to me and said, *Have you ever been with two women?*

Of course, I replied.

At the same time?

No. Just three months apart.

They both laughed at that.

Just at that moment, Jesus came over and told us that he and his party were just leaving. He asked the girls if they planned to leave with them. They looked at each other.

A minute later, Phyllis stood up to leave. Pam stayed put. Phyllis asked me what she owed for her drinks. I told her we'd settle in kind. She laughed and handed Pam a few bills. Background music: Rolling Stones' *Paint It Black,* handing off to Deep Purple and *Hush.*

Alone at last, I said. Pam smiled. *I really want you,* I continued, looking straight into her eyes.

Tell me something I don't know, she countered coyly.

Stephen Kleene has offered a proof of Kurt Gödel's 'incompleteness' theorem using basic conclusions in computer theory.

She stared at me, baffled, her eyes round in surprise. A few seconds later, she burst out laughing. She looked deep into my eyes and said:

You want to split?

She had barely finished speaking when I got up and took out my wallet to pay. I gave Mike two twenties, took my three bucks in change and we took off before she could change her mind. All this to the accompaniment of Aretha Franklin's *Chain of Fools*. I drove home in record time - thankfully, without running into any speed traps. I'd had a few drinks, after all, and I was speeding.

Fanouris was awake and heard us. When he opened the door and saw us, he just stood there, stupefied. Especially after seeing Pam, his jaw dropped – big time!

Hi! was all he could utter when I introduced her. He looked at me and asked in Greek where I had found her. I replied that I didn't know her, I just took her on consignment. I planned to keep her tonight, test her out and return her in the morning.

Pam and I got along just great. She turned my life inside out, to be frank, but in a good way. She made me forget all about Semy – and everything else for that matter. It was not just her otherworldly beauty and her fantastic body that amazed me, but her character as well. The complete package. She was solid, funny and good-hearted. She really was something else. It was as if the heavens had opened up the moment I first laid eyes on her and had conspired to bring us together.

As for Pam, she felt the same as I did. We were like two peas in a pod. She gazed at me as if she couldn't get enough of me. She pampered me. She was always taking photos of me. But I don't think we were ever in love. We were simply infatuated with each other, addicted even. And what really sent things soaring was the sex. She was genuinely hypersexual and insatiable. Unstoppable and without any taboos. And reluctant to put on any clothes when we were home alone. She wandered around almost totally naked, ready for anything. If I brushed against her, even accidentally, she would utter an aroused growl. I had never encountered anything like her before. It was with great difficulty that I was able to tear myself away to go to the university or even teach my classes. Lillian couldn't stand her but as for Fanouris, he was in cloud nine just because she was part of our group.

As for me, after a while being in her thrall, I began to protest, weakly at first, of course, but eventually, a bit more emphatically. She was crushing me. She had no respect for sleep, for simply relaxing, eating, anything. What the hell, was she bionic? Let alone how she was a maniac in bed. Fanouris, who was in the final stages of exam period, complained he couldn't concentrate. And he was right.

I told Pam to leave and come back in five days. No way. I sweated blood trying to persuade her. I told her it was about time she cracked open her own books a little because her exams were coming up soon. She said she was doing her clinicals and, anyway, she was a quick study. I wasn't sure what she meant but, in the end, I managed to convince her to go. I breathed freely at last.

I slept like a hibernating bear, ten hours straight. Then slapped together a beef stew. I bought a nice cut of meat, poked at it with a knife and slid garlic cloves into the slits. I browned it in olive oil with some diced onion. Covering it with water, I added nutmeg, cinnamon, cloves, and crushed hot peppers. I ground plenty of black pepper over it and let it cook for a couple of hours on medium heat. Then I added tomatoes and salt. I covered the pot, lowered the heat a notch and left it to simmer for another half hour. I accompanied it with some McCain's French fries. For dessert, I made a walnut cake infused with syrup, just like my mother makes. Fanouris, drawn into the kitchen by the aromas, kissed me, he was so excited.

I did a vast amount of work myself and even managed to get Fanouris to understand quantum mechanics. We solved a few problems together and he seemed to get it all. At the school, my classes were winding down. In the teachers' lounge, I wrote down the exam questions for each class, slid them into the special envelopes I was given, sealed them, signed each envelope and handed them all to Mrs. Lee, the secretary.

That Thursday, I thought the time had come to give Pam a call. We had been incommunicado all this time. I talked it over with Fanouris and he agreed. He asked me, though, to have her come back a day later because he had one more day of exams.

So, I went ahead and called her. She seemed happy to hear from me. But something in her voice bothered me. I mentioned this to Fanouris and we discussed it. We agreed that she had probably hooked up with someone else. Five days was a long time for her to go without some action. We both laughed.

She dropped by the next day. She was still a helluva doll. Unbearably beautiful. She was wearing a checked cloche mini skirt and a t-shirt. No bra. My heart started pounding like crazy the moment I laid eyes on her. Fanouris greeted her warmly, since Lillian wasn't around. She put her arms around me and gave me a peck on the cheek. I asked her if she wanted to sit in the living room or go to my room. I was hoping she'd prefer the second option. She shrugged and sat down on the sofa. Disappointing. I had coffee ready and offered her some. I asked her how she was and what she'd been up to over the past few days.

Roger came by, she said.

Right away, I realized what had happened. Roger was her high school sweetheart. He was studying architecture at Mississippi State University, the state she was from. She had told me that they had both agreed to keep their relationship an open one. Without commitments, without constraints. I remember I had told her, *Good for you!* impressed by her very modern attitude, given the times and the place.

Now she told me that he had come visiting and they had discussed making their relationship more binding. From now on, she was going to be spending some of the time in Jackson where he was studying, and the rest of the time he would be here with her. Our story together had come to an end. Worse, I would never have a chance to screw her again.

Fanouris, who had been coming and going from the kitchen all this time, at one point, winked at me and made a grimace as if saying, *Tough luck, that, but such is life!*

I got up and switched on the radio. Steppenwolf, *Born to be Wild.* It gave me the shivers. I poured a dose of bourbon into my coffee. I needed that. Pam watched me without saying anything.

Fanouris came in and said he was leaving for work at the supermarket. His exams were over. He'd get his results in a couple of weeks, but he wasn't worried. He felt he had done well, even in math which was his weak point. Pam kissed him on both cheeks, and I walked him to the door. I told him to give me a call during a break and that we could go out for a drink in the evening if he was up to it.

As soon as I had closed the door and walked back to the living room, my jaw dropped. Pam was on her feet, waiting for me, stripped naked. A goddess. She hugged me, then took me by the hand and led me to my room. *I Did It My Way* on the radio. Frank Sinatra. And that was the last time we ever saw each other.

I remembered that, several days later, I had this urge to see her again. I couldn't come up with an excuse to call her. What would I say? That I wanted to jump her for old times' sake – again? An idea came to me. What about asking her for those photographs she used to take of me? Then I had another idea, almost Machiavellian: I'd ask her to send me the photos with Phyllis. Wow! What a brilliant idea! I was impressed with myself.

I called her dorm and asked for her. I was told she wasn't in. Feeling the voice on the other end was vaguely familiar, I asked whom I was speaking to. It was Phyllis. I told her who I was, and she responded, *I figured.*

I told her what I had in mind and suggested she get hold of them and bring them to the bar where we had met. We could have a drink together, for old times' sake. She laughed and agreed. I was thrilled.

Four days later, she called me, and we arranged to meet at the bar at eight. She was on time. She walked in and immediately everyone's eyes turned to look at her. She was truly gorgeous, the very personification of beauty. I glanced at Mike who had a thumb raised as she passed by him to where I was sitting at the bar. I led her to a table at the back. Without saying anything, Mike came over and put our drinks on the table – a Manhattan for her, the usual for me. I've told you, the guy's a star. He had it all.

Phyllis talked about all kinds of things, even about her boyfriend. From her bag, she pulled out an envelope and handed it to me. The photographs I'd asked for. We looked at them together. They were really very good. Some were a bit too much because I was naked in them. I figured I'd tear them up later. She saw me blush and smiled. She asked me if I had ever had nude photos taken of me before. I said yes.

When was that? she asked.

A long time ago, I replied. *But then, my godmother came over and dressed me.*

She didn't get it and I had to explain. She laughed.

We talked about Pam. Phyllis asked what I thought of her. I told her that she was a great girl, very pleasant, principled and with a good heart. I said, too, that I was sure someday, she'd make some guy very happy.

Phyllis smiled and put her hand on my arm. She said she thought I was really sweet, and she liked me. She added that from the little she knew of me she could find no fault. What the hell, nothing at all? She asked if I had some secret failing. I nodded.

And what could that be? she asked, curious.

Photographs of my profile come out awful, I replied. She burst out laughing.

I offered her a cigarette, but she refused. I asked her if she just didn't like the brand. She replied that she rarely smoked and didn't feel like it right now. I lit up after asking for her permission which she granted with a smile.

All this time we were chatting, she sensed I was uneasy, that something was bothering me. She asked me what was wrong.

Something bugs me about you, I said.

What? she asked.

Your boyfriend, I replied.

She laughed at that. She asked if I was in a serious relationship back home in Greece. I told her no. I added that I had been involved with a girl who was older than I was, but it ended because her family objected.

Her parents?

No, her husband and her kids, I said.

She burst out into gales of laughter. The DJ was playing The Doors' *Riders in the Storm.* I asked her how her exams were coming along. She said that she had her last one coming up in a few days, but up to now, everything had gone well. Next year, she'd join the local hospital as an intern. She wanted to be a pediatric surgeon. I responded by saying I was proud to have met her. She smiled. I asked her if she wanted to leave. She looked at me, puzzled.

Why? Where to?

To my place, I said. *I'd really like to surprise you with a fabulous breakfast tomorrow morning*

She didn't say anything. Just looked me straight in the eye for a long time. The smooth, velvet voice of Elvis singing that incredible song of his, *Suspicious Minds,* played in the background.

Suddenly, she made up her mind: *Let's go.*

Leaving the bar, we headed for our cars. I held her tightly, my arm around her shoulders; her arm was around my waist. We made out for quite a while in the parking lot. I pushed her up against her car, kissing her passionately, and she responded totally, our hands groping, exploring each other's bodies. I suggested she follow me in her car. I led the way; she followed. But we never arrived at my place together. At a turn-off close to my place, she didn't make the turn after me. From my rearview mirror, I saw her speed up and continue straight ahead. I guess she had second thoughts. I was floored.

Myriad explanations ran through my head.: maybe she remembered she hadn't shaved her legs or perhaps forgot to change her undies, or that, finally, her southern conservatism had won out in the end. Whatever. For four or five miles, I'd been the happiest guy on earth. Flying high. But that sudden Scotch douche was a rude wake-up call, jarring me back to my pathetic existence. Shattered, I went to a bar close to home, a miserable dive I systematically avoided, full of shady characters, Standing at the bar, downed eight straight shots of vodka before dragging myself home on foot. An emotional wreck, not even bothering to change, I collapsed onto the couch in the lounge and passed out.

Fanouris told me, when we met again after all those years, that after I had left the States, he had run into both girls a couple of times, either together or on their own. Phyllis, he knew because Pam had once introduced them. Pam always talked to him whenever she saw him, and a few times, they had even had some drinks together. Sometimes she asked about me, wanting to know how I was, what I was doing, but, unfortunately, Fanouris had no idea of what I was up to. He also remembered how, the year before he received his B.Sc. degree, all three of them had ended up at the same

Halloween party together. Phyllis had been dressed as a Playboy bunny, and Pam had worn a catsuit. He told me they were the best lookers at the party. Pam was specializing in Neonatology and Phyllis in Pediatric Surgery. I smiled and thought to myself that those girls had finally succeeded in achieving what they had wanted. I asked if they still looked the same, like Barbie dolls. He nodded. He also mentioned that Pam had had a few flings with various guys at the university, but now was engaged to Roger and they were planning to get married the following summer at Roger's house in Ocean Springs, Mississippi, close to her hometown, Biloxi. I figured if they were still together, they must have been married for about 30 years already. Reasonable to assume Pam would be a grandmother by now! Suddenly I felt depressed. How many years had it been? How did fucking time fly by so quickly? Before Fanouris left the States to return to Greece after completing his Masters, he had run into Phyllis one night, at Mike's bar. She was on her own with a group of female doctors. Fanouris was with a girl he was going out with at the time, as Lilian was long gone, already married. When Phyllis saw him, she got up immediately and came over to chat. It seems she and her colleagues had been celebrating as exams were finally over, they had all done well, all receiving degrees in their specialized fields.

What did you guys talk about? I asked Fanouris, waiting for him to continue as he had paused and was just staring at me.

She talked about you, he replied.

Christ! I couldn't believe it. *Come on, man! Like what for example?*

She told me exactly what had happened with you that night, all those years ago, when she had suddenly left you and taken off in her car. She told me she had cried all the way to her dorm. She didn't know why she had left like that; it was a spur of the moment decision, something instinctive. Then she told me if I ever saw you again, to tell you that it had been one of her greatest regrets. She couldn't bring herself to call you after that. She was too embarrassed. She confessed this was something that had haunted her over the years. Many times she had wished she could have turned back the clock. That's what she said. And before she left - you'll never believe this - she looked me straight in the eye and told me to tell you that she loves you very much. No kidding. She even scribbled her home address on a slip of paper at the bar, for me to give you when I saw you. Naturally, I threw it away at some point. I didn't figure you'd expect me to hold on to it.

I sat there staring at him like an idiot, with my mouth open. What the hell had he just said? I couldn't believe my ears!

Are you sure that's what she said, you dumbass? You're not joking, are you? She actually told you she loved me? You're certain?

Yeah, you jerk! I've had this on my mind for years now. I guess, finally, all women are nuts! No other explanation. Because I remember exactly what you had told me about her, and because you were such a mess when I found you at home that night, that's why what she said made such an impression on me. Later, when things were calmer, I thought about this again. You know, after that, she had split up with the guy she was going out with in high school. She must have had it real bad. Must have fallen for you the first time she saw you. Coup de foudre, as the French say. Later, however, it seemed she chickened out, stepping aside when that other horny broad made a beeline for you and snapped you up for herself. Then again, later, when she had another chance. Who knows what she was thinking, dumping you like that in the middle of the road. Forever having regretted what she had done, it had weighed heavily on her. She needed to get it off her chest. That's why she came over and told me every-thing. Confession brings release, sets one free.

What kind of shitty life is this? I thought. What a fucking loser! I can't believe I'm just now finding out, at 60-something, balding and paunchy, that the most beau-tiful woman I ever met in my life was in love with me and I had never even slept with her?

What the blazes, my friend, you've ruined my day, I said. *Better if you hadn't told me. How will I ever survive now with all these memories? With all these questions, those 'why's and what-ifs' circling around my head, haunting me. I think I'll go kill myself now!* Saying that, I got up to leave.

Fanouris was visibly alarmed.

Come on, man! Cut the crap and sit back down. He even grabbed my arm.

I laughed and said, *OK, relax. I'll kill myself some other time!* Inside, however, I did feel a sense of vindication. At last, I was cured. The wound that cow had opened up when she left me high and dry in the middle of that road, had finally healed. After all those years of what I thought was rejection.

After all, I had been a very handsome Lothario in my day — a regular heartbreaker.

I ordered another beer for Fanouris and a vodka, straight up, for myself.

So now, back to our story.

I got my Master's accompanied by many accolades. I was told the official diploma would be awarded at a ceremony to be held in December at the University. They must have been pretty stupid at the least, to expect me to return, just to receive a piece of paper, considering it was a 12-hour flight from Greece. I told them I couldn't make it. They said there was no problem, it would be awarded *in absentia,* and the official degree would be mailed to me at my home address. They gave me a certificate indicating I had received a Master of Philosophy in Applied Mathematics, with Honors. I thanked them. Packed my many books, my records, and the rest of my belongings in a trunk and had them shipped to Greece. Then we sat down with Fanouris and had a long chat. He planned to hold on to the apartment. He had found someone to share it, another Greek who had come over to study physics. Fanouris had no plans to return to Greece; he'd stay in the States. I understood right away: the reason was Lilian.

Then we discussed money. He gave me $340, my share of the money we had paid to buy the stereo and color TV. He also reimbursed me for one of the two rents we had given in advance as a guarantee when we had rented the house. He'd get that back from the new renter. He'd also send me the money for my car when it was sold. I'd left it for sale at a used-car lot. I gave him all my sheets and towels. Also left him all my trainers, as we wore the same size. I went over to the church to say goodbye to Father Charalambis. I would miss that man. Two days later, after the Sunday service, from the pulpit, he announced my departure to the whole congregation. Afterward, when we were all gathered outside the church in the courtyard, everyone came over to wish me well, wish me success in my future endeavors, with the hope that I wouldn't forget them. I was moved. I'd miss them all. They were wonderful people.

On Tuesday, I left.

Barring all the friends I had made, what I missed most about America in all those years that followed, was the impressive organization and efficiency of the American government, its institutions and, by extension, all its services. I especially admired the separation of executive and legislative powers. This was the quintessence of democracy, just as in Ancient Athens. Also, in addition to the respect the people themselves had for every form of power, there was also mutual respect by the powers-that-be for the rights of the individual, the people. There was also respect for everything and everyone involved with education, from public school teachers to university professors. There was respect for public property and buildings as they were considered as belonging to all the people. The same held true for buildings on college campuses. They were protected by the police, as well as by private campus security personnel. No one could ever conceive of scribbling graffiti or defacing the exterior walls or the interiors of campus buildings. Bulletin boards were set up inside buildings for the announcement of any kind of information and could be used by any individual or group. All things functioned according to regulations and protocols. There were rules for everything. Every public institution or private company had an organizational structure with a job description for each and every one of their employees. There wasn't a single person, from the managing director on down to the cleaning crew, who didn't know precisely what their job entailed, where their responsibilities lay.

Most importantly, everyone understood their boundaries and never stepped over the line. Also, each and every employee, wherever they happened to figure in the hierarchy, whether in a key position or not, was evaluated on their work, their contribution to the common good, if in the civil service, or to their commitment to the goals and ideals of the company they worked for, if in the private sector. If someone didn't like that, they were always free to leave — that simple. Everything functioned smoothly, like a Swiss watch. The head of a department didn't have to be a 'star.' All he had to do was fill in that little box that determined the range of his duties and responsibilities. If he didn't fill it, there was always someone else ready to fill his shoes, take his place. In this way, the government functioned like clockwork, without having to depend on the smarts or the initiative of the employees. The system didn't depend on the individual, but rather, on group effort. The police reported to the mayor, who wanted his city clean, safe, and peaceful. Their slogan was *to serve and protect*, and, in my opinion, they did a very stand-up job.

On my return to Greece, the *Junta* was still in power. After visiting with my mother and sisters, I headed off to look up some old friends, or possibly a former girlfriend or two. I found my old gang at our favorite haunt. As soon as they saw me, they went wild! Shouts, hugs, kisses and the like. We were joined by Anestis, always the idiot, always a regular hanger-on.

What's up, man? He asked. *America, eh? What's life like in a foreign land?*

Foreign! I replied.

The rest of the jokers roared with laughter. Later, we decided to go to a bar on Fokionos Square, a place we used to hang out in occasionally. I didn't care for the music — too old school. I asked the owner at the cash register if he could play something new. He stared at me dumbly. He answered, *No.* I then suggested coming over every evening to DJ for 3-4 hours and play my own records, in exchange for free drinks. He said that wasn't in his interest. We took off. From then on, we only hung out at Apostolis' bar.

I joined the army. As the head of the family and only breadwinner, I was required to serve for only one year instead of two. The summons arrived in the mail, and I was to report to the artillery training center in Thebes. I found it easily. I won't bore you with stories from my army days, because they weren't all good. At the center, I ran into some of my old math colleagues. It seems we had all ended up in the same place, calculating trajectories for the greater good! However, after the first six weeks, when basic training was finally over, the time came for the selection of candidates for officers in the reserves, as well as for candidates for the Presidential Guard. No one approached me, as I was only in for the year. But some of my former colleagues were selected as candidates for the reserves. I saw them jumping for joy! What a bunch of rubes, being so ecstatic about wearing stripes, and then, for the last three years, a star! Beats me. If that's what they wanted so badly, why hadn't they sat for entrance exams to the Military Academy in the first place? Why not do things properly from the start? As things stood now, those asses would have to serve for a few more months anyway. Not that they cared much, as they'd be getting paid. So they said.

God is great, though.

The camp commandant happened to have a kid in high school, in 10th grade, and was looking for someone to tutor him in math and physics - a freebie, naturally. Searching through the bios of all the recruits, he dug up yours truly. He called me into his office to meet me and presumably to 'ask me if I was willing.' Naturally, I accepted. That was that. The end to all the hazing, the marching, and shooting for me. Every day I'd go over to his house on the campgrounds, to tutor his dumb kid. The good thing was that every day, his wife would insist I eat some of the delicious food she had prepared for the family, and so I no longer had to eat the Godzilla mystery meat that was served in the mess.

The commandant's son, however, was something else. A perfect example of *Homo Idioticus.* His IQ must have been around 40. The commandant, who was from Tripolis, a town in the heart of the Peloponnese was very smart and very much with it, and his wife was okay, too. Hard to understand how the kid had turned out the way he was! I wanted to ask if he was adopted but didn't have the heart. Now and then, the poor commandant would ask me how his son was coming along. I wanted to tell him 'just for the ride,' but I let it slide since the food was so great. Once, I recall asking his wife what the other tutors had told them about the boy, as I assumed they must have said something. Lowering her eyes, she confessed they had been told that the boy had a problem catching things 'the first time around.' Silently, I thought to myself, *neither on the second time around nor the third*!

Instead, I said, *The boy has potential, but he needs to work much harder, for much longer, and requires a lot of help from me. I suggest his summer vacation is spent revising geometry and algebra from the very beginning, to fill in the blanks, so to speak,* Or at least, so they don't show, I was dying to add.

The poor woman was so abjectly grateful, I felt sorry for her. It wasn't her fault her kid was a dummy. What could I say? I continued the tutorials with 'our' Minas for the remainder of the school year. Then during his summer vacation, we revised all the material once again, in great detail. Joking aside, he did in fact show signs of improvement. His parents found this very encouraging. The commandant was very generous in giving me extended furloughs, and I took advantage of the opportunity to go job-hunting in Athens since I was to be discharged in a couple of months. With these private lessons, I had secured the commandant's protection. This way no one bothered me when all that trouble with Cyprus and the Turks broke out. At some point, the situation with the fucking Atilla Lines and all that crazy shit calmed down somewhat. To tell the truth, I had been quite worried. When Minas returned to school that autumn, he chose to follow the program for applied sciences. The kid had balls, I'll give him that! No skin off my back, though I did give some thought to the poor sod who would be saddled with Minas when I was gone.

Finally, my time was up. I received my discharge. I went over to the commandant's house to say my good-byes. He wasn't around. He had his hands full since the Junta had fallen, and the situation was chaotic. His wife made me a strong, extra-sweet Greek coffee, served with an ice-cold glass of water, and treated me to a rosewater sweet. She asked me what I thought of Minas.

Are you from the town of Tripolis? I asked her.

No. From a village a short distance away, she replied.

I see. Do you have sheep? I asked her.

No, she said, gazing at me curiously.

You should get some! I said and saying goodbye, I left like a bolt of lightning.

I went out looking for work. I found a job right away at the Kanellos Cram Schools, just as they were about to move from Aristotelous Street to Solonos. I was hired to teach trigonometry. Algebra was taught by Mageiras, while geometry was the domain of another gifted young colleague. Up until I was hired, trig had been taught by Kanellos himself, along with Physics, his main subject, and he'd had his hands full.

I threw myself into my job with great zeal. I used the *Ferval* trigonometry textbook which, after *Tongas'*, was the very best there was, along with Kanellos' notes. I went over his exercises. They weren't anything exceptional, but they were very advanced. I liked them. I used a few and added some of my own.

The kids in my classes were all brilliant. Most of them were geared toward passing the challenging entrance exams for the National Technical University in Athens. We started out strong, with lots of enthusiasm. It was November, with the exams scheduled for June. A few days before the exams, I gave them a string of exercises I had selected for them to go over and absorb thoroughly. As it turned out, two of the exam questions were spot on, while a third had only a slight variation — a resounding success.

At the cram school, I was treated like a god. Old man Kanellos himself came over to congratulate me. All my kids received top grades. I asked for a raise and got it right away. Things were going well. I bought myself a blue VW Golf 1.5L.

It was round about that time that Aleka entered my life.

Aleka and I met one night at the cinema. End of spring, beginning of summer, I had gone to an open-air cinema, the *Verden* on Alexandras Avenue to see *A Streetcar Named Desire* with Marlon Brando. During the intermission, I got up to get a cheese pie and ran into Artemis. Artemis was a good friend of mine and an old family friend. She was the younger sister of Nonda, with whom we'd been classmates at school, and a friend of Eleonora, my little sister. She also happened to be a neighbor. We chatted briefly, and I suggested she come sit with me. She told me she had a friend with her and introduced me to Aleka. I took a good look at her. She was very attractive – a chestnut blonde with delicate features and beautiful honey-colored eyes. Tall, and with a super figure. A real beauty.

Glad to meet you, I said - and I meant it. Since I was there on my own, I went over and sat with them. After the movie, in my car, I took them for a drink at the *Green Park,* a posh open-air bar. On the way over, Artemis did most of the talking, telling Aleka everything. About my car, about America, my work, Nonda, Eleonora... She drove me nuts!

After we had sat down and ordered, we started discussing the film we had just seen. Aleka told me she had found it very moving. I asked her if she liked romantic movies, and she said yes. Then I asked her what film had made her cry the most.

A hot wax depilatory film, she replied. It was at that moment, I think, that I fell in love.

Aleka and I went out together a few more times, either to the cinema or some cozy bar. She had finished high school in Larissa and had moved to Athens to

118

attend university. She was now a third-year student at the Athens University of Economics and Business and lived in Kypseli, on Kerkyras Street. She and Artemis had met at the University. She asked me to go to the beach on Sunday, but I didn't really feel like it. When she asked why, I told her I never go swimming if the temperature on land isn't higher than my age. She asked me how old I was, and I answered 27. She said Sunday's forecast was for at least 30. She also told me to get over my hang-up, otherwise, the older I got, I'd be swimming less and less.

We went to the beach at Kavouri.

When she undressed, I noticed she had a stunning figure. She was wearing a white one-piece swimsuit that drove me wild. We went for a swim. I simply floated around as I'm not a particular fan of the sea. Aleka, on the other hand, plunged in and swam fast and far. For a landlubber, she did just fine. I asked her where she had learned to swim, expecting her to say 'in the Pineios River,' which flows through Larisa, but instead, she said in Agiocampos and Velika, two seaside towns.

She asked me why I didn't swim a bit further out to sea with her, and I said I wasn't a frigate. Why on earth should I sail out to sea? She told me swimming is very good for the figure. It helps one stay fit. I didn't buy that.

If that's true, I said, *then explain whales?*

She never broached the subject again. Then we went for a bite to eat. Fried fresh whitebait and salad, with some ouzo to wash everything down. It was nice. We got back late in the afternoon. I took her home, and she asked if I wanted to come up for a coffee. Of course I did, and not just for coffee. I needed to use the john. She lived on the fourth floor in a small apartment of about 650 ft2, a charming, tastefully furnished place, especially neat and tidy. I liked that and told her so. I asked her how much rent she paid. She said 400 drachmae. Good price. Later, she mentioned that she had also put two rents down.

Down where? I asked, and she laughed.

A bunch of open books covered the dining room table. I browsed a bit. One of them piqued my interest, a thick statistics textbook. I leafed through it. Nothing particularly special. Aleka went to make us some coffee. She had asked what I wanted.

To use the toilet, I said.

She laughed and said, *I meant what kind of coffee.*

American.

She didn't have any. I said I'd settle for a Greek coffee - extra sweet. When I came back from the john, we lit up a couple of cigarettes and drank our coffees. We chatted about various things. She told me she really liked me and that I had many good qualities.

There's something I must tell you. I have to warn you to be careful, not to push me too much because I fall easily, I said.

She laughed and leaned over and kissed me. That was all I needed. The safety was off. We spent two delightful hours together.

Later, there followed the usual small talk after sex. We talked about all kinds of things. Our families, for one. She told me all about her siblings and relatives. She told me one of her uncles lived in the USA. I asked her where, and she said Albuquerque, New Mexico. She asked if I knew of it. I said I didn't want to. She laughed.

Why don't you tell me something about your family? she said.

I have an uncle, I said — *my father's brother, who has no idea what he has.*

Lots of money?

No. Alzheimer's, I said.

She burst into laughter.

She told me when she was little, they used to call her Lia and she hated it. After the age of 10, she insisted everyone call her by her full name, Aleka. I didn't comment. She looked at me and asked what people had called me when I was a kid.

Up until the age of 10, I thought my name was 'go-to-sleep'! I replied.

She laughed and said she enjoyed being with me. She asked me to take her shopping the next day if I wasn't busy. I asked her what she wanted to buy.

I want to buy a slutty blouse, she said.

What do you mean?

One to go with all my clothes.

Laughing, I asked if she had a lot of clothes.

I have a closet full of 'I don't have anything to wear,' she replied

I realized I was really into her. I liked her a lot.

I told her that the following Sunday, as I felt I was suffering from a lack of Vitamin *Sea,* we should load up a cooler with beers, take the car and head for an off-road deserted beach I knew outside Attica where we could swim in the nude. She agreed. I was thrilled. And looked forward to Sunday when we would have the whole shebang to ourselves: *Beer, Sex and the Sea,* as the oldtimers would say!

With Aleka, we were together for five years. Good years. Great fun and mucho sex. I recall how she had driven me crazy about wanting to take me to Larissa and show me around. We never did go. Yeah, some big city! If you've ever seen the shithole of a town I had lived in in the good old US of A, what more was there left for me to see?

Aleka graduated from university and almost immediately landed a job in the Greek Parliament. I have no idea how that had happened. I remember her saying at some point that she had simply taken advantage of some of her influential connections. At the time, I didn't give it much thought. After all, we weren't seeing each other on a daily basis. More like once or twice a week in winter, while in the summer, what between vacations and my tutoring, we drew apart, seeing each other even less. I spent more time hanging out with my buddies from my old neighborhood, Victoria Square. Mostly with three of the guys who were friends from school as well as neighbors - Thanasis, Niko and Savas.

Thanasis was a civil engineer, and he worked together with his uncle, who had an engineering firm. He was the good-looking one — over six feet tall, of average weight, with straight black hair and honey-colored eyes. Great smile and perfect teeth. His father had a funeral home in the area and had buried practically everyone in the neighborhood.

Niko was a physicist and was a teacher at a high school in Vyrona. He resembled a heavyweight wrestler. No one would ever guess this guy could be a school teacher. From the time he was a kid, he was built like a tank: very broad shoulders, a thick neck and round head with closely cropped black hair. His facial features, on the other hand, were rather handsome; beautiful, gentle brown eyes, a pleasant smile, and shy expression. He wasn't as tall as Thanasis or me. Around 5'10". However, his appearance was impressive. He took up an inordinate amount of space. When the lot of us hung out together, no one dared bother us. One look at Niko and they'd hit the road. It was like having our own private bouncer around.

Savas was the best one of us all. He was a bit of a loafer. Other than that, he was slightly taller than Niko, at 5'11", but not as thin as Thanasis or me. He had the beginnings of a barely noticeable spare tire around his waist. He was very blond with hair straight as straw and blue eyes - rather Swedish in appearance. He resembled his mother, who must have been a doll in her youth. His family was very wealthy. His mother owned at least 12 apartments on Aristotelous Street, and at least that many elsewhere in the area - on Triti Septemvriou Street, Derigny, Hayden, and as far as Agiou Meletiou. She also owned two apartments in London's expensive Chelsea district and three more in Paris. All inherited from her family, an old Athenian political family. His father had a huge factory outside Athens that manufactured aluminum profiles. Practically the whole family worked there, except for Savas. His degree was in French literature, and he wanted to do something on his own. That's what he said. Now what the fuck it was he wanted to do on his own, he never mentioned. Maybe all he intended was to have a kid because he certainly wasn't capable of doing anything else.

Almost every evening we'd hang out at a bar owned by another friend of ours and old schoolmate, Apostolis. He had graduated from the Gymnastics Academy. He was a good-looking, tall guy, dark with an excellent well-toned athletic body, but he had a very long black beard, which in my humble opinion didn't suit him in the least. Why he thought it did, I had no idea. One day, I just had to tell him.

Hey man! It's ok to have a three-day beard, which happens to be a fashion statement, but not okay to look like one of the three Magi!

I remember he laughed, but after that, he did prune the beard substantially. Now, he looked cool. After his stint in the Army, his father, who owned the café, died suddenly. As the only son, it was his duty to take it over. But he transformed the place into a bar, turning it into a trendy venue. He was crazy about music and had a fantastic collection of LP's. In the beginning, he even DJ'd himself. Later on, he hired a young guy, Nonda, to take over as DJ.

We were staunch supporters of his bar, either starting out from or ending up there during our evenings out. It was a great place to chill - chatting and listening to music, joking around and having a few laughs. Our conversations usually centered around sex, cars, and football. Or the movies. In that order. We all had girlfriends. Only Thanasis' lady friend remained a mystery, as he had never introduced her to us. Naturally, we bugged him about it, but he always found some excuse or other. Only once can I remember him hitting on a chick, a girl from Vyrona who hung around the neighborhood. We saw them together once, and she looked just fine. I recall his VW beetle at the time was out of commission in the shop, and he was going to go pick up the girl from her house in his father's hearse. He'd come by Apostolis' bar before his date, and we kidded him about the hearse - even placing bets that the girl would never agree to get in. When he passed by the bar later that night, we were all over him to find out what had happened. He told us as soon as the girl saw the hearse, she balked. Didn't want to get in.

What happened then, man? Did she finally get in? we all asked.

She did, but only after a lot of grumbling, he replied. *'Are we really going out in that thing'? she had asked.*

Then what? we asked

Naturally, I told her she was nuts. Others, I said, are just dying to get in. That's what I said, and that shut her up.

Laughing a lot, we gave him a thumbs up, but that relationship didn't last long. In any case, if he did have something serious going on with someone else, we were never aware of it.

Savas was involved with Lily. A beautiful brunette from a good family. He had brought her over once, in the beginning, so we could meet her. He asked us if we liked her. I remember Thanasis telling him:

She's beautiful, but can she bake a pie?

Savas didn't answer, just stared at him curiously. Thanasis went on:

You loser, to be 'the one,' she's got to know how to roll out dough and make a pie. Any girl knows how to give blow jobs!

Savas chuckled, defusing the situation.

However, the fact of the matter was, Lily was too short for him. Only 5'3, the poor babe. This girl had set her sights on becoming an air hostess at Olympic Airways. At all cost. And Savas was proud of her, helping her with his connections as much as he could. One day, in a very good mood, he came by to tell us that the airline had finally agreed to hire her as a member of the crew.

The crew??? What crew, you idiot? I said to him. *Who are you kidding?*

I don't understand, he replied, frowning. *What do you mean?*

They'll never take her. She's too short. Barely over five foot, isn't she?

So? So what? he said. *They're all 'in on it.' They've all been paid off.*

She can't be part of any crew.
Why not?
Because she won't be able to see over the food cart.
He had a good laugh, too.
In any event, Lily did get the job.

Almost all of us were involved with someone. Niko had recently broken up with his girlfriend because she was pathologically jealous of him and had the habit of creating scenes right outside his school. Now, he had fallen for a girl named Iota, a new literature teacher at the same high school, three years younger, who was not interested in him and was giving him a hard time. But the poor guy was crazy about her. Head over heels. He talked about her incessantly. His love was driving us crazy.

Savas warned him to stop trying to hit on her because to get involved with a colleague at the workplace 'is an accident waiting to happen.' We joked about it but, nevertheless, that son-of-a-gun was miserable. Thanasis said to him there was no way she could be as gorgeous as he claimed. When we asked him why he replied:

Have you ever seen a beautiful Lit teacher, you guys? Do you remember any such a fanciful creature from your old school days? Eh? Of course not! They were all dogs!

We told him he was an ass as our high school was not the most representative example. Later, he dared us all to stand outside the School of Philosophy at the University to see if we'd ever come across any beautiful girls.

Don't be an idiot, I said. All schools include random samples of the population. You find all kinds.

Then he said:

Do me a favor and stop spewing all that mathematical mumbo-jumbo of yours! Okay then, let's assume that she's a beauty, as this lovestruck lump here claims - he pointed to Niko - but she's still bound to be surly and difficult to please, a regular sourpuss. No question about it. They're all like that. They can't fucking help it. Something is done to them at the University, and they come out this way. There's no other explanation.

It's a lot better, you ass, I said, that they're sour rather than sweet. That way, diabetics can fuck them, too.

At this, we all burst out laughing uncontrollably!

Nevertheless, Niko, the poor bastard, was inconsolable. He was drinking heavily and talking to himself a lot.

Do you all get what's happened to me? I've been beat by an iota.

Oh, cut the crapola, you bumpkin! We've been beat by even less and never bitched about it.

With a bit of this and a bit of that, we joked around, and time went by pleasantly. Truth be told, however, contrary to whatever Thanasis claimed, it turned out that the Lit teacher was no dog. She was beautiful, sweet, and good-natured. Tall, like Niko, but slim and shapely. Her face was doll-like, very pretty, and her chestnut hair was styled in a fashionable blunt cut which suited her perfectly. She had lovely almond-shaped green eyes. I liked her and had mentioned that to Niko when he had still been torturing himself over her, and he had been grateful, happy to hear it.

But, finally, at some point, Niko got involved with Iota. This lasted only five months. The bitch dumped him while they were still in the lovey-dovey stage of their relationship, to take up again with a no-good old flame of hers whom she had been head over heels with in the past. He was now back in her life, even though the guy was a piece of work and had given her a bad time. This almost killed poor Niko. The image he presented, if one disregards the tragedy of the situation, was laughable. To see this giant of a man pining away, reduced to such a miserable state, all in the name of love! We all tried our best to help bring him back to his senses, but nothing worked. He was inconsolable.

Savas had told him he was spoiling her to death, catering to her every whim, and had allowed himself to become a carpet for her to walk on. We had warned him to be more careful, less trusting, but he had ignored our advice. It was beyond his control, something he craved. I felt sorry for the big lug.

I tried reasoning with him:

Niko, my man, restrain yourself. Women want a guy to be a bit of a 'bad boy' to be attractive to them; otherwise, all they do is take you for granted. Be careful; I don't see this ending well. Take it from me. From someone who's been there.

Come on, Dino, he replied. *She's such a nice girl, how can I possibly treat the poor thing badly? I fucking can't. It's not in my nature.*

You fool, I said to him, *that's just the way God made women. It's simply how it is. Didn't you see what that whore Eve did to poor Adam, or that other bitch Delilah to that stupid idiot Samson? Tell me if I'm wrong. Didn't they deserve to be punished? And shall I tell you something else, so you can understand what loathsome creatures they are? Try putting a woman in a room with ten different guys and leaving her there for a few hours. Who's she going to end up with, eh? I'll tell you who. With the biggest jerk. The guy who will make her miserable in the end, make her cry herself to sleep every night. What do you think? That she'd choose someone like you? If you think so, you're a damn fool.*

We kept warning him, but he just wouldn't listen. When trouble came, I was afraid he'd end up doing something stupid. I discussed this with the other guys, and we decided we'd all keep an eye on him, in shifts.

Of course, you won't believe what finally ensued from that point on. The teacher's boyfriend ran out on her three months later, having in the meantime gone through all the money she'd been saving to buy a car.

Whereupon, she came running back to Niko, who she used as a backup. He saw this as a sign from above. Four months later, after she had made up the amount the boyfriend had run off with, the guy shows up again, and the stupid broad takes him back. Matter of fact, she even tried to skim some money off Niko to give to the sonofabitch. For a change, this time Niko didn't fall for it and refused to give her anything.

That's when we decided it was time for us to intervene. Thanasis mentioned that he was constructing a new apartment building in Byronas, near Niko's school. His foreman was a really tough guy from Crete, and he'd get him to get some of his boys to beat the shit out of the boyfriend. Savas argued it would be better if he got them to do that to the whore, not the guy. That's what he called her - a whore.

All this took place without Niko being present. This time, however, Niko wasn't acting as he had in the past. He seemed fine now. As if he wasn't bothered by what had happened. In light of this, Thanasis decided to put off taking any drastic action.

Niko and I had a special relationship as both of us had been in the Physics and Mathematics School together and had shared a whole lot of courses, even way back in high school. So I took it upon myself to pester him constantly, trying to figure out exactly what was going on with him. Despite my efforts, all I got in return was a few weak smiles whenever Iota's name came up.

What followed, of course, was to have been expected. The boyfriend took off again once he realized there was no more money to be had. The teacher came back to Niko like a wounded animal, begging for forgiveness. Niko welcomed her with open arms. He told her he had been waiting for her to come back. When he told us this, we lost it. Especially Savas, who declared the news made him want to rush over to a pharmacy, buy some poison and kill himself. Thanasis lambasted Niko; for brevity's sake, in essence, he called him a fool.

I, on the other hand, wasn't so sure what to think. And a while later, when Iota had strayed or said something she shouldn't have said - we never found out what - Niko beat the living daylights out of her. Yup. Niko. You won't believe it, but that's what he did; slapped her silly with his hands the size of shovels, really putting all his strength into it. He joined us at the bar and told us all about it. Savas called out to Apostolis and ordered a bottle of Dimple which we all drank down to the last drop to Niko's good health. Thanasis took us out that Saturday night to the *bouzoukia,* best seats in the house, to hear Voskopoulos - in those days, Greece's biggest star.

I ran into Iota in the street a short time later since we lived in the same neighborhood. I couldn't believe my eyes. She'd been on medical leave for the last fourteen days, recuperating. She still looked as if she'd been hit by a truck. After that beating, Niko didn't spend another moment with her. He was with us all the time as if nothing had ever happened. Whenever we asked how she was, he'd say, *I don't know, you guys. I haven't seen her. I'm sure she's fine. In any case, I'm sure she's not dead. She's alive.*

You'll be stunned to learn what happened soon after that. Iota stuck to Niko like a leech. An absolute slave. It was all, *Yes, Niko! Whatever your heart desires.* That sort of thing. She was a changed woman. Savas kept pinching himself to see if he was awake or in a dream. I recall asking Niko - confidentially, when it was just the two of us - if he ever hit Iota again. All he said was that once in a while, when they were making love, he'd slap her on the ass. I don't know what kind of look I gave him, because he quickly added that she liked that sort of thing. I never brought the subject up again — their business.

Later, I actually came to appreciate Iota, having seen her in a new light. When her old boyfriend rematerialized eventually, she reported him to the police for embezzlement, for having stolen money from her account.

She took him to court and managed to get her money back – with interest!

Two years after the beating, she and Niko got married. I was the best man. They've had two kids, a boy and a girl. The others baptized them: Thanasis, the girl, and Savas, the boy. Now, as I'm writing this, their son's just received his master's degree from LSE in London, is already working in a prominent shipping firm there and is about to get married himself. Their daughter is a lawyer married to one of her colleagues and has a daughter of her own, now two years old. We've gotten old, dammit, and haven't realized it. It's only when our kids grow up and have their own children that it hits you. That's just how it is. I'm sorry, but I've gotten carried away, and I'm all choked up. Let's get back on track.

Eventually, I got fed up with tutoring, even though I was making good money. I approached a couple of my colleagues, excellent mathematicians both, and after lengthy discussions, we decided to set up a research company. We all had the know-how in spades, as well as a hankering for something new, especially now that we were well into our thirties. We needed something different, something that wasn't yet established to any significant degree locally. Admittedly, we did start out cautiously. Politics was our initial target on which we aimed to base our business.

I enlisted Aleka, who had extensive connections in Parliament, to put us in touch with party leaders so we could present our ideas, how we aimed to extrapolate our experience abroad into the local arena. We managed to approach virtually all of them: Mitsotakis, Stephanopoulos, Kyrkos, Papandreou, Mavros, Zigdis, even Florakis. The first three were those that made the greater impression on me, but the others weren't far behind. From our discussions with these men, we gathered enough information to apply our own as well as existing mathematical models and offer them solid proposals. We presented them, and they were accepted. We were given the go-ahead by several of those party leaders to put our recommendations to the test on a trial basis. We did so and presented the results. As it turned out, we were spot on. That's how our business took off. Year after year, we kept growing, getting better. Several political parties put their trust in us, giving us quite a bit of business. In two successive elections, we provided the Interior Ministry with accurate prognostications. In the third, we were on Mega TV, commenting on the returns as they were pouring in. During the Athens Olympic Games in 2004, we had the idea of instituting an exit poll for the first time. That was it.

Our company had become one of the top firms in the business.

Aleka and I broke up after I found her *in flagrante delicto* with some guy in her apartment. We weren't living together. We each had our own place. I had bought myself an apartment in Kolonaki, 850 ft², on the fifth floor of a nice apartment building on Haritos Street. We had keys to each other's apartments, to make our lives easier. I've already mentioned that our relationship was flexible, and without a lot of baggage.

My colleagues and I were still in the process of building up the business. Endless hours bent over stacks of paper full of mathematical ratios and flow charts. We spent all our time in discussion, working out the fundamentals of our activities. In short, we were immersed in what we were doing, which was consuming us. After a 14-hour day, all I wanted to do was relax.

I dropped by the bar that evening, but no one I knew was there. Apostolis said the guys had just left. I called my mother and chatted with her for a while since Eleonora wasn't in. Danae, my other sister, by then had married and was living in Thessaloniki.

So, I thought of Aleka. Our first office was in the Ambelokipi area, on Sophia Schliemann Street. I tried to phone her a couple of times, but she didn't pick up. *Must be out of order*, I thought. I closed up, went down to my car, and drove off.

I reached her building and climbed up to the 4th floor on foot since the elevator had gotten stuck on the 6th. I could hear music through the door. Good, she's in, I thought. The bedroom was off to the left of the entrance hall, with the living room straight ahead, and the kitchen and bathroom to the right. When you entered the apartment, if the door to the bedroom was ajar, you could see right in. And I did, that day. I saw her, naked, straddling a hairy guy who looked like a bear. I was kind of shocked, but so were they when they saw me – a scene right out of an Italian bedroom farce, like the ones Nino Manfredi and Vittorio Gassman used to make. Aleka was the first to recover, leaping off the bed and closing the door. A few minutes later, she emerged and came up to me, wearing one of my nice American t-shirts and her gym tights. She asked me not to make a scene, something I had no intention of doing anyway.

We stared at each other for a while.

Then I said, *Isn't that my t-shirt you're wearing?*

Yeah.

How come it fits so nicely?

I washed it, and it shrank, she answered.

When you washed it, were you drunk? I asked. She laughed and asked me if I wanted it back. I said no.

I handed her my set of keys to her apartment that I was holding and asked for my keys back. She fetched them and handed them to me. I turned and left. As I walked down the corridor, I heard the door closing behind me.

She called me the next day, and we met for coffee in Kolonaki. She apologized. I didn't accept it. She said, *I know, I'm a bitch.*

I didn't reply, but I was thinking to myself, *Yeah, right! Whoring can be such a tough business!*

Then she said, *You know, I'm just playing the field, I'm not waiting for my Prince Charming.*

I told her that's fine because a prince might turn out to look like Charles. She laughed. Said she didn't want us to end up estranged. She said she had been kind of swept off her feet by that hairy guy - as if I gave a damn that he was hairy or why she had gone with him. I replied that being swept off your feet was fine - as long as it wasn't by a truck. You had to be careful there.

She laughed. She said that it was only with me that she laughed so much. She asked me to give her something of mine as a souvenir. I searched my pockets for a moment and said, *Here! Take this hemorrhoid ointment.*

She laughed but didn't take it. We parted company. I paid and left for the office, carrying with me all the years we had spent together. It turned out to be tough without

Aleka. The lack of sex hurt. I didn't have much free time on my hands to go out on the prowl for any, so I was feeling its absence. I remember once, one of the guys asked me how I was for sex and all I could say was:

Man, the closest I've been to sex lately was this very morning when I was buying cigarettes at a kiosk. I gave the proprietor a 10,000 drachma note (equivalent, say, to a hundred-dollar bill in those days) and he said, 'Thanks, buddy! You've gone and screwed me!'

Thanasis suggested I join a gym. Lots of girls signed up at gyms. Savas disagreed, saying only fat chicks signed up. Thanasis called him an ass. Most girls who went were real lookers, trying to maintain their figures. I listened to their banter but said nothing.

Speak up, man! Thanasis said. *Why don't you say something? You don't like my idea?*

No way! I said. *You jerk, gyms are like museums. You can watch, but you can't touch. What good's that to me? Watching those tight-assed broads prancing around in their leggings when all I end up taking home is my work?*

Savas had just come back from France where he had gone on business. Or so he said. We didn't believe it because Savas and business didn't really go together. His mother must have sent him to Paris to oversee some repair job on one of her properties there.

Anyway, he told us that he was shocked to see the swarms of Moslem women wearing burkhas that had flooded the streets of Paris. We couldn't quite picture this because at that time, sights like that were nonexistent in Athens.

Thanasis butted in to say, *How confusing it must be for a guy to have his wife and daughter constantly wearing burkhas.* Puzzled, we asked him what he meant.

Grinning, he said, *The danger is the guy might accidentally sleep with his wife!* He had a point there!

Savas also described some weird bars which had opened up in Paris featuring buck-naked French chicks doing all kinds of shit by themselves or with each other right there on the stage. We listened to him with mouths agog. You see, the Iron Curtain had not yet lifted to allow the flood of Svetlanas to storm into our part of the world for every sex-crazed guy to fuck.

Thanasis piped up again telling us he had recently seen some video porn that was absolutely insane:

There was this six and a half foot tall broad who took a bottle of vodka and pushed the whole thing up her twat.

Come on, man, Niko said, his voice hoarse.

Pretty wild, isn't it? Thanasis said, looking him in the eye.

Dammit! Niko said. *And vodka is my favorite drink.*

We roared with laughter.

But all of this was of little help to me and my woes. In my desperation, one evening, I wandered into one of those dives in Plaka. I have no idea how I ended up there. All I can remember was that it was raining and inside, there was great music playing, the place was full of girls, and the drinks were really exotic. I think I had gone on my own. I remember sitting at the bar, nursing a second cocktail when I glanced at the girl sitting next to me. A real looker. I tried to draw her attention. She turned toward me and asked:

Something wrong?

Have we just had a fight? I asked her. She looked at me in surprise.

Of course not, she answered, taken aback.

So why the silent treatment? I asked. She laughed and looked at me closely.

I'm in love with you, I said.

But I'm a lesbian, and I'm with someone, she replied.

I'm in love with both of you, I said, not about to give up so easily.

You're too late. By a few years, she said, chuckling. But she did accept the drink I offered her.

I realized that I had no chance of scoring in this place. So I decided just to have some fun, at least until the rain stopped. I remember a brunette with short hair and pretty eyes came up to the bar next to me to order. I asked her what she was.

I'm a lawyer, she said. I looked at her closely.

And what's your name, my dear?

Maria-Louisa, she answered.

Putting on a solemn face, I said, *Now tell me that you have four tits, just to finish me off.*

She smiled broadly, took her drink and walked off.

Another brunette, tall, really gorgeous this one, with short hair, came and sat next to me. Had this sort of wild beauty. Giving her wet hair a shake, she plunked her bag on the bar between us. She called out to the bartender, who obviously knew her, to bring her a shot of whiskey. I kept staring at her.

And what's up with you? she asked me aggressively. I wasn't fazed.

I really dig you, I said.

Fuck you! she replied.

That's what I had in mind, I said.

She laughed.

Taking her drink from the bar, she also left to join her friends.

The bartender stared at me persistently, obviously wanting me to order another drink. I nodded, and he rushed to bring me another. As he put it down in front of me, he leaned over and asked me, *What sign are you?*

The fish, I replied.

Fish with what?

With oil and lemon dressing, I said.

He laughed. *I'm a Capricorn, Taurus rising, with Venus in my fifth house,* he said. I had no idea what he was talking about.

So, when are you expecting your period? I asked him.

He grinned and moved on.

What the hell? How in the world had I ended up in a place like this?

I recall another occasion, when Savas was especially jumpy. We asked what was wrong, but he refused to say. A few drinks later, though, he sat next to me and, leaning over, told me in confidence what was bothering him. It seemed that this French friend of his he was putting up had brought these weird cigarettes with hash with him and was pressuring Savas to try one. Savas was hesitant.

Tell me, he said. *With grass, I've heard that it's like you're in a world of your own and you don't know what's going on around you. Is that true?*

All you're describing to me, you jerk, is the Communist Party, I responded.

He looked at me dubiously but said nothing. I don't know if he tried the hash or not, after all.

On yet another occasion, I found him in an agitated state. There had been a mix-up with the telephone connections, and he had ended up speaking to some stranger, some girl. But he liked the sound of her voice, so he didn't hang up. It sounded so fresh, he said, and musical. Anyway, after a long chat, they arranged to meet. He asked her where she lived, and she said she lived in Glyfada, at the other end of Athens. Not very convenient. He asked her how old she was, and she said she was 25. That was better. So far, so good. They decided to meet halfway, at the Tomb of the Unknown Soldier, in the middle Athens. He asked for her name, and she said it was Joanna. He asked her how he would recognize her.

I'm 5'6" and weigh 140 lbs. How will I recognize you?

At that point, Savas paused.

So, what did you tell her? I asked him, intrigued.

I said I'd be the one holding a tape measure and scales.

I told him that he had made my day. And when I told the story to the others when they finally showed up, they all busted a gut laughing.

We laughed a lot in those days, it's true, but as for the 'other thing' – nothing! I was near earning a black belt in 'nofuckee.' In December, before Christmas, Thanasis, with both of us in a heightened state of inebriation, suggested I write to Santa to bring me a chick. I took the bait.

Santa Claus is for kids, you jerk. For us older folk, it's more like claus-trophobia, I said. They did stop bugging me about the sex thing after that.

It was around that time that I met the woman I married.

We were looking for a secretary for the business and prospects had been coming in for interviewing either by me or my two colleagues. Whoever was available.

One day, in walked a stunning, five-foot eight brunette with beautiful green eyes and a body to die for. Aliki, our departing secretary, asked me if I had time to see her. I said to check with the others because I was in the middle of something and was busy. Aliki replied that they were both out, so I told her to show the woman in. Needless to say, I hired her on the spot. After a week, she finally stopped addressing me formally because it had started to bug me, all that 'mister' and 'sir' business.

We were working together one day when I turned and asked her:

How old are you?

Twenty-two, she answered. *How about you?*

Some days I feel as if I'm hitting heatwave levels. She laughed.

After work, I'd take her and we'd go out to one of the 'in' bars in the area. We'd have a few drinks and chat about anything that came to mind. After a while, I remember that our conversations gradually became a bit more personal. Eventually, she asked where I stood on sex.

Usually, I'm standing with my ear to the ventilation shaft listening to the newlyweds on the floor below going at it, I replied. We both laughed a lot at that.

Another time, she asked me if I had ever been with a prostitute.

For five years straight. Until I finally realized it, I said.

After about two months of this banter, I suggested she come up to my place.

Why? she asked.

I want to show you my sketchpad, I told her, and she came over.

We had a good time, and we clicked.

She was from a good family. Her father was PR director at PPC, the power company, and her mother worked for an insurance outfit. She had one brother, five years younger, who was somewhat of a problem because he was quite a handful.

Once, when he was finishing the 11th grade, I asked her: *Is he a good student?*

He's got a good mind, but he just doesn't study, dammit!

What's he into?

He's into going off to the islands for some fun, she replied. That cracked me up.

For her birthday, I wanted to buy her a wallet I knew she had seen and liked. I went to the shop where she had seen it. The salesman came up to me and asked if I needed any assistance.

I pointed to the one I wanted and asked, *How much?*

Twenty-seven thousand drachmae, he replied.

Funny. It doesn't look like it has so much money inside it, I said.

He howled with laughter.

In any event, I did buy it for her, and she liked it – a lot more than she let on. I even went back to the same shop and bought one for myself. Not quite the same one; instead, one a bit more modest and less expensive, but just as nice. Of course, after all that spending, for a long time, I was broke, with nothing left to put in my new wallet.

Two years passed. We'd been spending most nights together. One night, we were lying in bed when she farted. The poor girl, I remember how she blushed a bright red, ashamed, and buried her face in her pillow, her voice muffled as she apologized again and again. I stroked her back and told her not to worry; farting was completely natural. She didn't respond.

Anyway, sweetheart, in a relationship, farting is like a solitaire, I added.

What do you mean, 'solitaire'?

A diamond, silly! It makes it all official!

I remember, we laughed a lot at that. And soon after, we decided to get married. We were in the middle of moving our offices in those days, to larger premises near the US Embassy. She was two month's pregnant on our wedding day with our older daughter, Stefanie, who is now 25 and in her final year as a post-graduate student at university. After giving birth, Iphigenia returned to the office, working for another two years before having our second daughter, Angelika, who, now, is also at university.

In 2010, having outgrown our offices once more, we moved to premises further downtown, off Syntagma Square. My partners and I had gone out to dinner with our wives one evening, just after we had published our company's balance sheet to celebrate when my wife commented that we owed our success mainly to the women present.

Behind every successful man is a woman, she said with a grin.

Then I'm glad we're not gay, I remarked. *Because behind every gay guy is another man.* We all had a good laugh over that.

Mitsos, one of my two partners in the business, piped up and declared:

Let me say that I think that behind every successful man is a confused former girlfriend who considered him a total asshole.

That was a good one.

It was around that time that Fanouris who, if you remember, had gotten in touch with me a while back and got my heart doing cartwheels over Phyllis. You haven't forgotten, have you? Anyway, he was calling to let me know he was with Elias. Elias, if you remember, was the guy who had skedaddled out of town in the dead of night, way back when, to escape young Helen's father's wrath for having sullied her underaged body with his seed, and who Fanouris had told me was now an MP with the Socialist Party. Remember, now? Anyway, Fanouris was having coffee with him at that very moment at a café off Syntagma, if I was interested in joining them.

I'm on my way, I said, and took off.

I was really pleased to meet up with Elias after all these years - some 37, give or take. He had changed, as had we all. I was now bald, and so was he. Fanouris had been spared that. But Fanouris had a belly; as did Elias. Not me, though. But I had let my beard grow. So had Fanouris, but not Elias. That's how it had turned out: two out of three permutations, always shifting.

I kidded Elias for being bald.

At least, your hair isn't falling out any longer, I told him.

He confessed that he had begun to go bald over that business with Helen. He asked me when I had started losing my hair.

I don't remember exactly when because when I started to shed, I thought I was just changing into one of those beautiful Angora pussycats, I replied. We all laughed.

We talked about everything under the sun, remembering every little detail from the past - what we ate, communion, Father Charalambos, Lilian, the other guys at Uni. Everything. We commiserated over Petros' death. Then we got into politics. Elias mentioned he had gone over to George Papandreou's party, the left-of-center PASOK, but he wasn't feeling good about it and was thinking of switching. In any event, he was a leftist.

I lost it. *Leftist, you asshole? From my point of view, or yours?* I asked him.

They both burst out laughing.

I asked him if he knew Aleka. He did. He asked me how I knew her. I told him she and I had been together some time back. He laughed.

Bit of a whore, that one! he said.

I asked him why he meant by that, and he answered that she gets laid by at least twenty of the 300 MP's with each change in the government. I was shocked.

Wow! I guess she's a bit like FYROM.

What do you mean?

Well, I'm the only one who calls her Aleka. Everyone else calls her a whore. That got a big laugh.

In any event, I continued, *It's odd that she's managed to grow as tall as she has.*

They looked at me. *What are you getting at?* Elias asked.

Since she's always getting jumped, how in the world did she manage to grow at all, you jerks? More laughter.

Man, I always enjoyed your sense of humor, Elias said. *I remember the good times we had at your place, plenty of good food and lots of fun.*

You're damned lucky I could cook better than your mother! I said to him.

Elias asked me if I still had my collection of vinyl. I told him I still had them all and played them once in a while.

We got to talking about our families. Elias had married twice and had a son from each marriage. The older one, he rarely saw, he was studying abroad. The younger boy was studying at Athens College.

Wow! Nothing but the crème de la crème for your boy! Great leftist you turned out to be, you fraud! I said.

What's so wrong about that? There's no crime. I'm just taking advantage of the system, he retorted.

I told him I had two gorgeous daughters, still in school. University. He asked me what they wanted to be.

The older one wants to be a model.

Model? What model?

A Ford Focus, I retorted. *'What model?' You jerk! Do you know many types of models? Anyway, I'm just joking with you. She's going for a degree in tourism.*

We had been laughing so loudly that customers at the other tables had begun staring at us. He asked me how my girls were doing at the University. I told him things were different now. Nothing like how things were when we were there. In those days, the Greek universities were still schools. Now, they're more like a bordellos.

No, I corrected myself quickly. *At least, a bordello has a modicum of rules, a sense of order.*

They asked me what I meant. You see, both of them had only studied abroad. I told them of the mess Greek universities were in now, courses being constantly interrupted halfway through the school year, having to be made up later after consultation with the administration. Student Council elections. Student factions – stuff Elias was aware of but was keeping mum about. I told him he had better put aside his 'leftist shit' and all the rest of it and do something about the situation.

The conversation turned to the subject of our wives. Both Fanouris and I declared ourselves to be faithful husbands. Elias, on the other hand, hesitated.

I'm an unrepentant lover of the fair sex, he finally blurted out. Those were his exact words.

Right! As if we're repentant, I retorted.

We parted company after exchanging phone numbers, promising to stay in touch.

I've forgotten to mention that I have five incredible nephews and nieces. Three are Danae's kids, the other two, Eleonora's. Oddly enough, Eleonora married – Thanasis, of all people. That's right! Surprised? Imagine how surprised I was! It turns out they had been together from our high school days, when he was in my senior class, and she was in ninth grade. That's why he had kept it from us, the rat.

I remember being upset when they first announced their relationship. Pissed off, I called Thanasis a pedophile – and an asshole. But quite soon, I calmed down, and everything after that was milk and honey. Best man was Niko, who was accompanied by his wife, the former Lit teacher who, by now, Thanasis was fully aware. was definitely no sourpuss.

After Eleonora got married, our mother was living on her own. I no longer stopped by for a meal as I used to in the past, when Eleonora was there to cook. Now, my mother would often forget herself on the phone, chatting with her daughters, her grandchildren or her friends, her food on the stove in the kitchen burning to a crisp more frequently than the garbage bins on the Technical University campus.

Once, she fell and broke a leg, as happens so easily at that age. We rushed her to the hospital for hip surgery. When we brought her back to the house, we hired a woman from behind the Iron Curtain to watch over her. That was a big deal in those days — these women who came from abroad and looked after our elderly saved a lot of people.

I went and bought all kinds of equipment to help my mother out in her condition– special items for the toilet, for the bath, a wheelchair, crutches, a walker, and all the rest. She was recovering nicely. After a while, the woman we had looking after her called to tell me my mother wanted me to get her a cane so she could finally get rid of the crutches and the walker.

Because I was exceptionally busy at work at the time, I asked one of our employees to pop down to one of the shops near the hospital that sold that kind of stuff and buy a cane for my mother. He looked at me and asked:

To help her walk?

No, you imbecile! So she can weave a basket! I yelled at him, on the verge of throwing something at his head.

My mother lived for several more years, long enough to welcome great-grandchildren. When she died, we had her cremated. That's what she wanted. She'd always been advanced for her time. We kept her ashes in a large alabaster vase in our living room before eventually casting them into the Mediterranean Sea as was her final wish.

Sometime later, I brought in workers to paint the house. As they were covering the furniture with plastic sheeting, one of them picked up the alabaster vase, looking to put it down somewhere safe. I took it from him and gently placed it under a table. He asked me what it was.

My mother's ashes, I told him.

She sure smokes a lot, doesn't she?

I didn't respond to that.

I remember my mother often. One of many memories of her that stands out is that she always carried a fan in her purse. When I was just a kid, and I happened to annoy her, she'd take it out and start fanning herself furiously like switching it to max.

I'm really happy with my family life. I'm still madly in love with my wife, though she complains that I don't pay much attention to her needs any longer. And I do mean her sexual needs. Or so she says. I tell her she's got it all wrong, but she counters, saying she's judging me by my actions – or lack of. In fact, just the other day, she told me she intends to advertise in the personals for 'a tall, dark, unshaven youth to wring my breasts after I come out of the sea.' I managed to talk her out of it.

As for my daughters, aside from being truly beautiful, they're both also top students. The older one, Stefanie, being more bookish, got into her school of choice right away. God forgive me, but her looks remind me a bit of Pam.

My younger daughter, Angelika, an olive-skinned beauty, was interested in Sociology and was accepted at the University of the Aegean on the island of Mytilene. However, she soon changed her major to Psychology. She enrolled at Deree, the American College of Greece, though she didn't abandon Sociology entirely, maintaining her enrollment at the other university long distance, hopping over occasionally to the island for exams and such – and returning with a supply of that fabulous *pastourmas*, a salted and cured beef which Mytilene is renowned for.

When they're around, we have lots of fun. They both have a great sense of humor, especially the older one. I remember once when Stefanie was still in high school, I kept asking her if she needed any help with her homework.

Desperate, I finally blurted out, *So, what about chemistry?*

Well, there is some between my boyfriend and me, she replied.

Tears came to my eyes.

One winter, we had all gone up to Kalavryta to ski. We stayed at a great hotel in adjoining rooms, both with fireplaces. The one in our room started smoking. I called down to reception and made a fuss. Suddenly the door connecting the two rooms opened and in walked Stefanie to see what all the commotion was about. I told her our fireplace was smoking.

Go tell its mother! she quipped. I cracked up.

While at Uni, she became involved with a fellow student, as tends to happen at that age. From the beginning, the two of them constantly fought. She'd close herself up in her room, and we could hear her yelling at him on the phone. She must have been driving the guy crazy. Her mother and I looked at each other, mystified.

Finally, one day, after she had hung up on him, I walked into her room and asked point-blank what was going on.

He keeps doing stupid things, dad. He's like a child, she said. *I'm just trying to knock some sense into him.*

Why are you trying to change him, girl? I asked. *Why don't you just dump him?*

What!? And leave him as stupid as I had found him?

I didn't have an answer to that.

As time passed, it seems the boy must have straightened out because everything suddenly turned to honey. My daughter was now always with her mobile in hand, texting with him. Whenever I was home, I would just sit back, watching her with a silly smile on my face. Her mother found that hilarious.

One afternoon, I found Stefanie in a particularly foul mood. I asked her what was wrong.

He's not answering any of my messages, she said. *Either he no longer loves me, or he's dead. God, it had better be the latter.*

Alarmed, I crossed myself several times.

On another occasion, Angelika and I had had a tiff. For some time, we weren't even speaking to each other. After a while, though, she came to me and said:
I don't like this. I don't want us to be like this.
So, what do you want? I asked her sternly.
Ice cream, she replied.
How could I possibly keep a straight face after that!

Now that they're all grown up, the three of them, mother and daughters, can sit together for hours, gabbing away. Talk, talk, talk. Once in a while, I break in uninvited with a comment, and all hell breaks loose. Especially when the subject is 'relationships'; they will not accept any interference from me. As if those two girls of ours had been brought to us by a stork, or some other form of immaculate conception.

I recall asking Angelika once what she looked for in a relationship.
Everything! was her answer
What do you mean? I asked, curious.
A cellphone, computer, drawers, a wallet. Like I said! Everything!
I made it a point never to ask that again.

Later, I tried out a variation. I asked her what she expected to gain from a relationship.

Ideas for the next one, she replied.

My girls love me, and I adore them. When I get home from work after a long day during those times when we're desperately trying to meet a deadline at work, the first thing I do is take a long shower. After that, I sink into my armchair in the living room and smoke a cigarette, watch a little TV, and chat a bit with the wife.

Right away, Stefanie comes up to pamper me.

Can I bring you a drink? she asked me the other day.

Tom Collins?

Sorry, papa. No can do. I broke up with him last week, she replied.

I didn't say a word. Grinning, I got up, went to the kitchen, and mixed the drink by myself.

Just the other day, Iphigenia and I were getting ready to go out. She was sitting on the side of the bed, staring at the clothes in her closet. Both daughters came into the room to ask her something, but she was unresponsive. Stefanie asked her what was wrong.

I don't know what to put on, my wife replied.

Why don't you try putting on the radio? came the reply. Her mother scrambled around on the bed for something to throw at her but found nothing.

Last night, I came home late and found Angelika watching TV.

What's on the box? I asked her.

Dust! she replied.

I left the room.

Later that evening, she came down and told me the toilet was running.

So, what do you want me to do about it? Run after it? I replied.

Later, I was sitting in the living room watching TV. My wife was out, Stefanie, somewhere else, lost in space. I was feeling a tad peckish. Angelika was on the sofa, painting her toenails.

I said, *Hey! Why don't you fix us something?*

Sure, she replied.

So, what do you have in mind to fix?

My hair.

I fell off my armchair laughing.

I got up, went to the kitchen, and made myself an omelet.

This morning, over breakfast, Angelika told me I should create a Facebook page. *No way!* I declared. I told her that I belonged to the generation that used to demonstrate in the streets of Athens, demanding the destruction of files and profiles. Last thing I wanted to do was intentionally open a file on myself for all to see. Sheer idiocy!

She insisted that Facebook was absolute magic. I didn't understand what she was getting at, and I asked her what she meant.

Well, look at it this way. With each 'like' on your ex, you get yourself another ex.

Stefanie and Iphigenia roared with laughter. I didn't get the joke. Only after they explained it did I understand and agreed that it was pretty funny, after all.

I tell you all this to show how deeply ingrained humor is in our family. At the very least, it's something that's never lacking. Everything else might be missing at one time or another. At times in the past, money's been short; at other times, sex, and at yet others, happiness. Or time enough to enjoy the simpler things in life was hard to come by; or good company, as friends moved away. At times, just having a good time was difficult and, occasionally, even vacations were out of the question. And so on. We always tend to miss what we lack. Never satisfied. And now, with the current economic crisis, we lack what we once had, and don't even have the energy to remember what that was.

The only things I continue to enjoy are a good drink, good company, cooking, and smoking. The drinks, we continue to enjoy at Apostolis' bar, in our old neighborhood. We may have all scattered in different directions and live far apart, but that's where we still gather. We have a grand time, horsing around and laughing to our hearts' content.

Just the other day, we were all gathered there, celebrating Thanasis' new car, a secondhand Porsche. At one point, Savas suddenly said:

I've decided to write my daughter in English. We all stared at him, aware that Savas and English were never on the same wavelength. We waited for him to continue, but all he did was take out a sheet of paper and write 'my daughter' on it and hand it to us.

We all had a good laugh over that.

On another occasion, I remember, Costas, a friend of ours, an electrician, was planning to open his own shop in the neighborhood. He came looking for us at Apostolis' bar one evening to talk to us. He wanted our help in coming up with a catchy slogan for his business cards. I suggested he writes '*Let us remove your shorts*'. Everyone loved it.

Thanasis, in the meantime, had recently joined a popular local group lobbying for the British Museum to return the Elgin marbles to Greece. He tried to convince us to enroll as well. Savas and Nikos did join. I was reluctant, as the new Acropolis Museum had not yet been erected. They were very pushy about it and I didn't like it – and I said so. They asked me if I had ever been a member of some group. I told them that just two years ago, I had joined a support group for procrastinators – but we hadn't met yet.

Ingrained habits and good company are givens. And cooking is another mainstay of my life. Whenever I get a chance, I cook, if just for the fun of it. It relaxes me. Smoking, however, is in crisis mode. The doctors keep telling me I've got to stop – and I resist. Everyone else in our circle has quit. Savas, who recently married Amelie, a smashing Greek-French beauty, after Lily had dumped him to marry a pilot, quit smoking last year. Thanasis quit after Eleonora insisted the smoke was bothering her. Niko was never much of a smoker anyway and found it easy to stop altogether. Now, the only remaining smokers in the group are Iota the teacher, my wife, and me.

I must admit, though, that today's cigarette packs are genuinely repulsive. You buy one, and you're exposed to all kinds of shit on them. Just the other day, Saturday afternoon, we had all gathered outside Apostolis' bar as the weather was really fabulous. I hopped over to Pavlos' kiosk on the corner and asked for a pack. When I returned, I looked at the packet and read the warning: 'Smoking can result in erectile dysfunction.' That shook me. I leapt to my feet and ran back to the kiosk.

Dammit, Pavlos, I cried out. *Take this pack back and give me one that warns about cancer. I don't want this shit.* Cancer, you see, we're used to. Doesn't make that much of an impact any longer.

I sit back once in a while these days and think of how the years have gone by, and how everything's changed. I admit that I know nothing. It's like going to the movies, falling asleep in the middle and waking up not knowing anything about the film and how much time had passed.

When I look back, everything seems different. After all, I had been around when they still had school uniforms in public schools. Now, almost everything has changed. All the years that have gone by have left their mark on us. Some visible, others invisible to others. The thing I hate most is when I see an old person and suddenly realize we had been in high school together. Now, what I find hard is not finding what I want but finding out where the hell it is.

You see, we're not young anymore. We're all now between 60 and over the hill. This isn't so bad since the original plan was to die young – as late as possible! I see some of my friends, widowers living alone, trying to date. It's pathetic. Dating at our age is like going to a garbage dump and looking around for the least broken and disgusting object!

But let me tell you this. There's one thing that has never stopped whirling around in my head: we grew up with the Doors and ended up with Windows! I think that says it all. Weird stuff, I tell you.

After all this, I've gotten hungry. I look at my watch and see that it's ten in the morning and it's Sunday. Everyone else is asleep. Outside, it's a beautiful day. An autumn Sunday, sunny and warm. Only in Greece will you find such light, such fabulous colors.

I give a little thought to what I can dish up to satisfy my hunger. I recall something I had read in the cookbook *Bostanistas* that had made quite an impression on me. Time to give it a try, I say to myself. I put down the newspaper and my glasses on the glass table on the balcony and go into the kitchen.

I found what remained of yesterday's country-style bread and thought to myself, this is perfect. I cut four thin slices, placing them on a sheet of alufoil. I slice three nice, juicy tomatoes in four and add them to the foil. I sprinkle a little olive oil over everything, add salt and pepper, and slide everything under the grill. When the bread slices crisp a little along the edges, I turn them over.

From the refrigerator, I take out some feta cheese and a small cup of creamy *katiki* cheese. I plunk some of the feta and a tablespoon of the *katiki* into a bowl and mash them with a fork, making a paste.

Removing the bread slices from the oven, I rub them on one side with a garlic clove and sprinkle them lightly with a little olive oil and salt flakes. I remove the tomatoes from the oven and arrange them on a plate. Putting everything on a tray, I take it out to the balcony. I spread each slice of toast with the cheese mixture and top off with some of the roasted tomato. I go first for the slices with the browned edges. I stretch out my hand to the pot of thyme hooked onto the railing. It's nice to be able to reach it without having to get up.

I take a bite and right away, I feel better. What a feast!

I get up and pour myself a tall glass of the *Pitsiladi* ouzo Angelika had brought me from Mytilene and throw in a single ice cube. I sit back down. I feel like the lord of the manor. I enjoy my snack while everyone else is still slumbering.

My mind starts playing tricks on me, traveling suddenly way back, way, way back and far, far away…

Smiling, I close my eyes briefly and then light up a cigarette.

THE END